A
DANGEROUS
IDENTITY

ALSO BY RUSSELL FEE

FICTION

The Sheriff Matt Callahan Mystery Series:
A Dangerous Remedy, Book One

Russell Fee writing as Russell Ó Fiaich:
Who You've Got To Kill

POETRY
A Dash of Expectation

A DANGEROUS IDENTITY

A SHERIFF MATT CALLAHAN MYSTERY

RUSSELL FEE

BOREAS PRESS

Copyright© 2019 by Russell Fee
All rights reserved.

No part of this book may be used or reproduced in any manner whatsoever including Internet usage, without written permission of the author.

Published by Boreas Press, Oak Park, Illinois

ISBN: 978-0-9985119-3-1 (ebook)
ISBN: 978-0-9985119-4-8 (paperback)

Cover design by Erik Offerdal
Cover photo © by Joan Flynn Fee
Book design by Maureen Cutajar

For
Heather, John, and Patrick—
who fill my heart with unbounded joy

We are what we pretend to be, so we must be careful about what we pretend to be.

—Kurt Vonnegut, *Mother Night*

It is the basic condition of life, to be required to violate your own identity.

—Philip K. Dick, *Do Androids Dream of Electric Sheep?*

Chapter 1

@/@

T HE GIRL DIDN'T HAVE her head on right. That was for sure. Seeing how it lay by her side, face down in the sand, as if trying to hide from the sight of her body, which was nude and posed on the beach like a pole dancer about to spin, one leg thrust out, the other crossed over at the knee, back arched, an arm flung above what would have been her head. She had already attracted an eager audience when Sheriff Callahan arrived.

He nudged his way through the crowd until he was at the body. "Everyone, move back, way back," he said and knelt on one knee. He hovered over the body without touching it, surveying it and the sand around it a moment before he called out to the onlookers. "Okay folks, show's over. Everyone, clear out." He stood and eyed the remaining gawkers to make sure they knew he was serious. They did and began reviewing the photos and videos they had taken on their cell phones as they walked away. Callahan figured the poor girl would be on Facebook and YouTube within seconds. He crouched down on his haunches for a closer look.

Apart from her decapitation, the girl had not died well. Deep slashes crisscrossed her body nearly severing her limbs and exposing her internal organs. Callahan was amazed she didn't lose more than her head. As he took a closer look, a shadow snaked over him and settled across the body. Callahan turned and looked up. Dr. Carl Remy was staring down at him. Remy held half a sandwich in his right hand and a rolled, grey blanket under his left arm. He bent down and took a bite of his sandwich. Callahan heard the lettuce crunch.

"Hmmm," said Remy. "Boating accident. Probably spun through the props of a yacht, judging by the size of her wounds. Either fell overboard or was diving, I would guess. Probably fell overboard. That would explain the lack of clothing. Wild parties take place on some of those yachts. I'll check her for drugs and alcohol. Here, cover her with this." Remy tossed the blanket to Callahan. "Might as well protect what little dignity she has left if the ghouls start sneaking back for another look before the ambulance gets here." Remy nodded toward the people down the beach, most of whom were watching them.

Callahan stood and shook the blanket open to its full length with a quick snap and let it float down, guiding it over the girl. "You got here fast," he said.

Remy took the last bite of his sandwich and wiped his hand on his trousers. "I was in the area having lunch with a friend when Julie called and said you wanted me over here—fast. Came right away."

"Thanks," said Callahan. "I don't know how long she's been here or how long between the time she was first discovered and someone finally called the station. Around fifteen minutes ago, Julie got an anonymous call. That's all I can tell you." He swept his hand over the body. "From the look of things, a crowd gathered here for a good while. The sand has been disturbed all around so it's impossible to tell if she was dragged here or washed up from the lake. There were high winds and waves last night." Callahan took his hat off and wiped his forehead with his bare hand. He had begun to sweat. "A bit unusual to have her severed head next to her body, don't you think? If she washed up on the beach, you wouldn't expect her head and body to have stayed together in the rough water."

"Unusual but not impossible," said Remy. "If a yacht ran her over not far from shore, the waves may have pushed her onto the beach before her head washed away from her. Also, if she was wearing clothes, maybe the shreds entangled her head and kept it with her body in the water long enough for them both to wind up here."

Callahan gazed down the beach. "Then where are the shreds of clothing?" he asked and wiped the sweat again from his face.

Remy shrugged and said, "You look a bit green around the gills. You okay?"

Callahan ignored the question and said, "Are you good on your own for a few minutes? I want to question some of our audience; see if anyone knows something that might help us find out who she is and how she got here."

"Wait a minute," said Remy, laying his hand on Callahan's shoulder.

"What?" said Callahan, twisting toward him.

"Aren't you going to turn her head around and look at her face? Maybe we'll recognize her," said Remy.

"Well, I was hoping that . . . seeing as you're the county medical examiner . . .," Callahan didn't finish the sentence.

"Oh, I get it now. You want me to do it. That's why you got me here so fast. Fine," said Remy. He fixed Callahan with an unsympathetic look and pulled a pair of latex gloves from his back pocket. He stretched them over his fingers as he lowered himself above the girl's severed head. "Let's just examine the skull first," he said and began parting the hair over the rear and top of the skull. "Doesn't appear to be trauma of any kind." He placed a hand on either side of the head. "Upsy-daisy," he said and raised the girl's face out of the sand. He rolled her head over until it was on its side and, still holding it between his hands, rotated it with three, quick, delicate tosses until it faced up. Then he gently laid it back onto the sand.

Callahan and Remy stared down at a face that held none of the horror its owner had experienced. Her facial muscles were not slack but relaxed, her eyes were gently closed, her lips held the last trace of a sweet smile. She looked as if she had just received a cherished compliment.

"Well, I'll be damned. That's Susan Gibbons, the kindergarten teacher's aide at the school. What the hell was she doing on a party yacht?" said Remy.

*   *   *

Callahan left Remy alongside the body to perform a more thorough onsite examination, take pictures, and wait for the ambulance while he took names and questioned people on the beach. It became obvious that he wouldn't get any more information from the crowd about the body than he had gotten from his own observations, but he extended the questioning for as long as he could. The truth was that he felt strangely affected by the scene and glad to be away from it. Certainly, there was the revulsion and accompanying waves of nausea at the condition of the corpse, but he'd seen death in enough forms in his previous life as a homicide detective with the Chicago Police Department to handle that. Perhaps it was her youth or the way her body had betrayed her in its odd dismemberment and public humiliation. Or her peculiar serenity after what must have been bedlam. Or the thought of how much her family would suffer at her gory debut on social media. Maybe at his age death was becoming too familiar, too close. He couldn't put his finger on the cause, but the feeling was unfamiliar and unpleasant.

Callahan considered the change in him since coming to the island and wondered if his current mood had anything to do with it. Seen on a map, Nicolet County formed a speck thirty-five miles off the west coast of Michigan in the middle of one of the Great Lakes: tiny, remote, and insignificant to all but those few who lived on the island. He included himself among those few. He had come to think of himself as an islander now. Horribly mutilated and disfigured in a vicious attack as a detective, he had retreated into a lair of anxiety, despair, and isolation—until the island. The island had given him Julie, Max, Amanda and a life with purpose.

That was it, he thought. He was experiencing survivor's guilt. He had found a new life on the island, but the girl on the beach had lost hers in the water off its shores.

He needed a distraction.

Chapter 2

CALLAHAN DECIDED THAT HE needed company to help shake off his malaise and so headed home from the beach to pick up his two favorite companions and take them to one of his favorite spots on the island. It was also one of theirs.

As he drove, he marveled again how the past and present competed in a horse race for the island's identity, with the past a full length ahead. The island's Irish heritage had been preserved for almost two centuries. Each successive generation of the Arranmore fishermen who settled the island had nurtured its roots until those roots were intertwined with the fabric of the island's culture. Callahan couldn't turn in any direction without seeing evidence of that heritage in the names of restaurants, hotels, pubs, streets, bays, and people; or in the cemeteries, churches, entertainment, traditions, and even the language of the island. The local moniker of *America's Emerald Isle* fit the island perfectly. Ireland was everywhere and had engendered in him a renewed interest in his own

Irish roots. When he pulled up to the house and honked, Max and the dog ran out the door.

∗   ∗   ∗

The path dropped and rose like a crumpled blanket through the trees along the serrated stretch of dunes that spread behind Blue Spruce Bay.

It was midday, and the leaves split the vertical rays of sunlight into thousands of speckles before they hit the forest floor. Max spread his bare arms out and watched the dappled patterns whisk over his skin as he walked. "Cool," he said. Then Max stopped. "You okay?" he asked.

"Yeah, sure. Why?" said Callahan.

Max didn't answer but started walking again.

"I was just enjoying the quiet," said Callahan. "I needed to think."

"I like quiet," said Max.

"I know," said Callahan.

Just then the dog appeared on the path at the top of the dune in front of them. It checked to make sure Max and Callahan were still behind it and then turned and disappeared again.

"What were you thinking about?" asked Max.

"My job," said Callahan.

"I think about my job too," said Max.

"Tell me about it," said Callahan.

"Ellen. She likes TV. I sit with her. She cries when I must get up. I tell her I will be back, but she still cries. Sarah likes cards."

"Do you play cards with her?"

"Yes. No." Max shook his head.

"What do you mean?" asked Callahan.

"She gives me cards, and I give them back to her. But that's not playing cards. I try to teach her, but she doesn't want to learn. Maybe she will."

"Tonight, after dinner, do you want to play some cards?" asked Callahan.

Max looked up at Callahan and smiled. "Sure."

"Speaking of work, your shift at the Adult Daycare Center starts in less than an hour. Your mother will be mad at us both if you're late. We'd better head back to the cruiser," said Callahan.

"Yes," said Max; and, within seconds, the dog appeared at Max's side.

The dog and Max had developed some sort of mental telepathy between them. Callahan had to call the dog repeatedly before it came to him, but, without bidding, it showed up whenever Max wanted. Callahan couldn't figure out how Max did it. Most of the time, Max and the dog were inseparable.

∗   ∗   ∗

After dropping Max off at the Adult Daycare Center, Callahan decided to stop at the harbormaster's office on the way back to the station to ask about yachts sailing to or near the island. The harbormaster answered him by taking him out to the end of the pier and pointing into the bay.

The tiny dark red dot shimmering above the gleaming white of the luxury yacht's upper deck was visible for almost a mile out to the mouth of the bay.

"Here," said the harbormaster, handing Callahan a pair of binoculars, "take a look."

Callahan took the binoculars and adjusted the focus until the dot became a figure wearing red pants and a white polo shirt. The figure stared back at Callahan through its own pair of binoculars. Callahan lowered the binoculars and passed them back to the harbormaster. "Who is that?" he asked.

"The yacht belongs to Anthony Bland. Don't know who that is on deck, but he's been there off and on all day. From the way he's dressed, he's not a crew member so he must be a guest of Bland's. That means he's got money, lots of money," said the harbormaster.

"What's he doing here? Our island, as nice as it is, isn't exactly a billionaire's vacation paradise," said Callahan.

"He's not on vacation. He's probably prospecting," said the harbormaster.

Callahan waited for the harbormaster to explain, but he didn't. Instead, he turned away from the bay and began walking back to his office. "Just heard the radio signal. That's probably a boat calling in," said the harbormaster.

"Wait," said Callahan, trotting after him. "What's he prospecting for?"

"That yacht has been docking all along the Michigan coast for the past month. Jet setters like Bland and his guest don't take cruising vacations along our Midwest Riviera. They wouldn't stoop so low. My guess is there's something out there they think will make them money. They're looking for it."

"Any idea what that might be?" asked Callahan.

"Not a clue," said the harbormaster.

Chapter 3

THE YACHT WAS MASSIVE and sat solidly moored inside the bay, impervious to the waves that jounced the other boats tethered to their buoys or anchored near shore. Its great distance from any other yacht was an affront to the usual nautical amity expected from sailors of the Great Lakes and a clear signal to the curious that their attentions were unwelcome. If Callahan needed any confirmation that the owner wanted privacy bordering on isolation, he found it in an inability to communicate with the yacht. Only silence greeted the harbormaster's repeated attempts to make radio contact.

Amanda Gillespie, Callahan's deputy, spotted the first crack in the barrier wall surrounding the yacht. She immediately called him at the station. "Sheriff, a launch from that yacht just dropped someone off on shore who got into a waiting SUV. I recognized the vehicle. It belongs to Tony Bland. You know of him, right?"

"Of course," said Callahan. "The island's first resident startup genius."

"And wealthy survivalist whose home here is a veritable bunker. Huge also. I've only seen it from a distance. The house is set back a good distance from a wire fence that borders the entire property," said Amanda.

"Well, you're about to see it up close. I want you to go out there now and interview Bland about anyone who has been on his yacht in the past month. Get the names and duties of the crewmembers and a list of guests with the dates and times of their visits."

"Right on it," said Amanda.

*   *   *

Bland's home defied the popular perception of a survivalist's bunker or at least Amanda's idea of what one should look like. There was no attempt to hide its location or camouflage its purpose. A one-story steel and glass structure, it sprawled over two acres of an open field, more like the first floor of an office building rather than a comfortable vacation retreat. It was also surrounded by a low stretched-wire fence that provided no protection from intrusion but which functioned well as a warning to others to keep their distance. The structure invited curiosity but nothing else and was a source of resentment on the island. Bland had used no labor of any kind from the island for its construction but had imported all labor from the mainland.

Amanda drove the cruiser up the gravel entrance road to a wide gate and stopped. She could see no microphone or speaker for communicating with the home, but the gate was not locked, so she swung it open and drove the cruiser through it. She traveled until the gravel road disappeared into the grass in front of the house. There was also no walkway to the front door. Someone had driven the SUV up to the entrance of the house and parked so that it blocked a direct approach to the doorway.

Amanda got out of the cruiser and walked to the entrance, edging herself the few feet between the SUV and the door. She reached for the doorbell, but before she could press it, the door opened and there stood Tony Bland.

"Are you collecting donations for the sheriff's re-election campaign?" said Bland.

"No," said Amanda, somewhat taken aback.

"Then I'm afraid I can't help you with anything," he said and shut the door.

Amanda stood stunned in front of the door for a few seconds before she began pounding on it. She then held her finger on the doorbell button. She could hear the continuous buzzing inside. But Bland did not reappear.

*　　*　　*

Amanda spun around and retraced her steps in front of Callahan's desk for the fourth time. She'd come into his office agitated and angry about her skirmish with Bland.

"If you keep pacing like that, you'll wear away the carpet. If we had a carpet," added Callahan.

"Okay, so if he's not hiding something, why wouldn't he talk to me?" asked Amanda.

Callahan shrugged. "Bland's conduct does raise suspicion. At this point we can't force him to cooperate with our inquires. He apparently knows that. But he wasn't being very smart. He's piqued our interest in him. Also, it's only a matter of time before he'll need our services. We'll see how uncooperative he is then. In the meantime, find out everything you can about Susan Gibbons."

Chapter 4

ABROAD BRUSH PAINTED Susan Gibbons as young, white, middle-class, and moderately ambitious. The only child of a father who owned a car dealership and a mother who managed a real estate office, she had grown up in Kalamazoo and graduated from Western Michigan University with a degree in education two years ago. Her parents had died in a car crash shortly before she graduated. Her first, and only, job had been as an aide to the kindergarten teacher at the island school. She was well-liked by the principal, teachers, and staff, although considered somewhat shy. The principal had described her as being introverted but wonderful and outgoing with the children. She came to the teachers' social gatherings—Friday happy hour bar visits, birthdays, weddings or baby showers—but had no close friends and no significant other. She lived alone in a rented cottage on the island. She did not own a car but walked or rode her bike to school. The last persons to see her were two teachers she said goodbye to after finishing one glass of chardonnay at O'Malley's Pub on the Friday before her discovery on the beach. No one had any idea how she wound up nude and mutilated in the sand. That had been the extent of the report Amanda prepared for Callahan. He had not been satisfied. He wanted more depth. So, she had put down her brush and picked up a scalpel.

* * *

Anne Meara's apartment was testament to a blend of thrift, ingenuity, and style. A teacher's salary in Nicolet County floated well below the level of a king's ransom, yet Anne had managed to decorate her apartment with tasteful and expensive furnishings. The steady resale of vacation homes on the island provided resourceful islanders with a trove of gently used furniture at bargain prices. Anne had obviously been very resourceful. But she looked out of place, even in her own artfully appointed home. She was tall and thin and had an angular and elastic body that seemed to bend and twist to impossible degrees. When she beckoned Amanda into her living room, she screwed her torso around so that she almost faced backwards and swept her arm even further toward the couch where she asked Amanda to sit. Amanda tried to put the image of an insect out of her mind. When Amanda sat down, Anne excused herself to make tea for them. When she returned, she offered Amanda a cup and then sat in the cushioned rocker with her back erect, knees together, and her mug of tea resting in her lap. Amanda leaned back on the couch.

Before visiting Anne, Amanda had questioned her and two other teachers in the teacher's lounge at the school about Susan Gibbons. The group interview took place because all three teachers had a free period while each of their classes had specials such as gym and music. Amanda wanted to get background information about Susan and learn the extent of the teachers' familiarity with Susan's life. But convenience had trumped thoroughness and maybe opportunity. In retrospect, Amanda realized what she had overlooked in the interview. Anne's individual awkwardness or discomfort in the presence of the police now seemed a reticence to be forthcoming in the presence of the two other teachers. Anne maybe knew something about Susan that she was unwilling to reveal in public. Amanda had berated herself for her lack of diligence and was now making amends.

"So, you like island living," said Amanda.

"It's different. It takes a while to get used to, but, yes, I like it. I like the school and teaching. The kids are great," said Anne. "Plus, my boyfriend is from the island, so I have another reason to stay," she added and smiled for the first time since she let Amanda into the apartment.

"What about Susan? Do you think she liked living on the island? It's not for everyone," said Amanda.

Anne hesitated and then said, "At first maybe. Anyway, she never complained. That is until about a few months ago."

"What did she complain about?" asked Amanda.

"Nothing specific. It wasn't even complaining, really. She just left the island a lot. Whenever she got the chance. She'd say she needed to leave. That's all."

"Did she tell you why?" asked Amanda.

"No. I figured she had a boyfriend on the mainland or was looking for another job. You know, something like that. We were friends but not close. We did socialize occasionally, but Susan was hard to get to know. She didn't talk much about herself." Anne leaned down and placed her mug on the floor. "Sorry," she said. When she sat back up, she was quiet as if thinking.

Amanda was about to ask another question when Anne spoke again.

"There was something though. Something she told me. Something strange that was out of character for her."

"What?" asked Amanda.

"She said she was going to the Caribbean, Aruba I think. I thought she should be happy about it, but she wasn't. She seemed worried. More than worried, actually. She told me that she had planned a short trip but that if something changed, she might not come back. At the time, I didn't think much of it, just that she might want to stay down there or finally leave the island permanently. Most people not from the island don't stay forever. But now I don't know what to think. It was the way she said it—hesitant like. I guess I should have asked her about it. I don't like to pry, so I was waiting for her to tell me why. But she didn't." Anne was silent again for a moment and then said, "I'm not being too helpful, am I?"

Amanda didn't address Anne's concern but instead asked, "What made you think she was worried?"

"It was the way she acted: quiet, but nervous at the same time, like she was arguing with herself about whether she should say more. That was the feeling I got." Anne reached down to pick up her mug but leaned over the wrong arm of the chair. She became confused when she couldn't find the mug on the floor. "I . . . I . . . I'm sorry. I'm just being silly, I suppose."

Anne sat back up in the chair. "Would you like some more tea?" she asked.

Amanda stood up. "No thank you. One last question: Do you know if she had any close friends either on or off the island?"

"No, I don't. She kept pretty much to herself. No one came to visit her as far as I know, and she never spoke of anyone that she was close to—at least not to me."

Amanda reached into her shirt pocket for a sheriff's department card with her phone number on it. She handed the card to Anne. "Here, please take this and call me if you think of anything else about Susan you can tell me."

Anne took the card and continued to stare at it for a moment as she got up from the chair. She then looked up at Amanda. "I'm so sorry about Susan," she said.

＊　　＊　　＊

When Dr. Carl Remy spoke of the dead, he voiced stories of their departures from this world—the ones that death gave them the courage to tell. There was no sadness in them, no regret, not even horror, only factual renditions of inevitable endings touched with resignation and occasional whimsy. But in that telling, the circumstances always revealed the dead for whom they had become, the secrets beneath their disguises disclosed. Remy had seen enough death as the county medical examiner to become a master storyteller.

Amanda had read Susan Gibbons' autopsy report several times but wanted to hear her story from Remy personally. As usual, Remy appeared to have slept in his clothes or picked them up from the floor and thrown them on, rushing out of the house. Disheveled didn't even come close to describing his sartorial taste. Most of the time his wardrobe included a white doctor's coat, which hid some of the damage from view. But not now. He adjusted his ample posterior in his chair and then leaned forward, clasping his hands, and resting his arms on his desk.

"Would *sliced like a grilled kielbasa* be too graphic a description for you?" he asked.

Amanda winced.

"Thought so. Then it's best you not see the body. It's something you won't forget."

"I understand that it's your opinion that she died in a boating accident—caught in the blades of a large motor boat. Is that right?" asked Amanda.

"Yes," said Remy.

"Could she have died by any other means that you can think of?" persisted Amanda.

"No, because there is no evidence of an intervening or contributing cause. The nature and pattern of her wounds are consistent with a boating accident. Even her beheading fits with that cause of death. In other words, she was not beheaded first and then dumped overboard and run over by a boat. And she didn't drown first. The post-mortem findings just aren't there. There was some water passively present in her lungs, but that would naturally occur when a body has been in the water for a while. And there was no anoxic cerebral injury." Amanda looked puzzled. "Her brain was not deprived of oxygen as it would have been if she drowned," Remy explained.

"Oh," said Amanda.

"Also, I've just received the results of the blood tests from the toxicology lab. She had no recreational drugs or alcohol in her system when she died." Remy hesitated for a moment and then said, "I do have another opinion that isn't explicitly stated in the autopsy report."

"What is it?" asked Amanda.

"I've noted that she was sexually active. That's the clinical fact. What it hides is that our young lady had more pricks in her than a dive bar dart board," said Remy.

Amanda looked confused. "I don't get it," she said.

"She displayed the physical evidence of an extensive history of sexually transmitted diseases."

"Oh," said Amanda and, despite herself, blushed.

Remy noticed but didn't address her embarrassment. "I've not seen prostitutes with the long-term punishment she's taken," he continued.

"You think she was a prostitute?" Amanda was stunned.

Remy shrugged. "Maybe . . ."

Chapter 5

CALLAHAN STOOD IN THE hallway outside the wall window of the Adult Daycare Center's dining room and watched Max feed a wheelchair-bound guest. He spooned the pureed vegetables into the elderly woman's open mouth and gently scooped what dribbled down her chin as she closed her mouth and swallowed. He then touched her lips with a cloth napkin. She smiled. Max smiled back and offered another spoonful to begin the cycle again. Callahan was charmed—there was no other word for it—by Max's slow, deliberate caring and the bond it engendered between him and those he attended to at the Center.

Julie had been a double surprise for Callahan, first popping up as the dispatcher at the station and then becoming much more. They had fallen in love, a circumstance that had been improbable and baffling for them both; and not the least because of Julie's age and Callahan's horrific disfigurement. But Max, her son, had been the astonishment for Callahan. Max had Down syndrome, but

Callahan discovered that Max's world was not shrunken by a hampered understanding of it. Instead, it was expanded by a selflessness unblemished by conceit or want. He was a revelation and a treasure.

Callahan waited until Max finished feeding the woman and then entered the dining room and walked over to him.

"You ready to go home?" he asked.

The woman's eyes widened and darted back and forth between Max and Callahan in an anxious quiver.

"Adele needs to be in the lounge now. She likes to watch TV," said Max.

The woman relaxed and smiled.

"Sure," said Callahan. "I'll wait for you outside in the cruiser."

"Yes," said Max.

*   *   *

"This isn't the way home," said Max. He was looking out the window of the cruiser, watching the landscape whiz by.

"We're going home but by a different way," said Callahan. "I want to check something out first."

Max turned to Callahan. "What?" he asked.

"Some people think they're above the law and—"

"What does that mean?" said Max, interrupting Callahan.

"You say that about someone who believes they don't have to follow rules or act in a way that is good for everyone, only for themselves. Do you understand?"

"Mr. Fink is like that at the Center," said Max.

"Exactly," said Callahan. "So, there is someone new on the island that I think is like Mr. Fink. I want to see if it's true."

Callahan turned off Orchard Road and onto the gravel lane that led to Bland's bunker. He braked to slow the cruiser, letting it grind over the drive at almost a snail's pace.

"You can help me," said Callahan.

Max sat up and slid his hands down the tops of his thighs. Then he looked at Callahan expectantly.

Callahan swept his hand across the view outside the windshield. "The person who owns this land might be doing something here that he shouldn't or allowing something to happen here that he shouldn't. I need you to help me find out what that might be. Okay?"

"Okay," said Max, beginning to look around outside the cruiser's window.

Callahan pressed the button to lower the driver-side window and, as the window slid down, he heard the report of a rifle followed quickly by two others.

"There," said Max pointing straight ahead of him.

Callahan stopped the cruiser. "Where?" he asked.

"There," said Max, his arm outstretched, pointing over the roof of the low building in front of them.

"I don't see anything. What are you pointing at?" said Callahan.

"There, over the trees," said Max.

Callahan followed the trajectory of Max's finger and saw a stationary black spot against the blue of the sky just above the trees behind the bunker. The blot began to enlarge and become more defined as Callahan watched, mystified, until he realized it was coming toward them, not with the swoop of a flying bird, but straight and unwavering as if aimed at them. Just before it reached the cruiser, Callahan recognized it for what it was—a drone. It stopped and hovered a few feet from the windshield and then quickly rose and disappeared.

"That's not right," said Max.

"No," said Callahan, "I don't think it is."

Chapter 6

"IF THE DRONE IS Bland's and if he is using it to hunt or to harass hunters, then he is breaking the law and could face jail time and a hefty fine. Michigan Compiled Laws Section 324 says exactly that." Amanda tapped her computer screen and then pushed her chair back from her desk and turned to look up at Callahan.

"That's a string of *ifs*," responded Callahan. "Let's start with the hunting. What can be legally killed this time of year?"

"Don't have to look that one up. It's open season year-round on coyote, feral swine, porcupine, opossum, weasel, and some common small birds. That's about all you can legally hunt now, and you need a license for most even if you're hunting on private property," said Amanda.

"July obviously isn't trophy hunting month. Nothing in that list sounds valuable enough to risk using a drone to hunt."

"Unless he were hunting bigger game out of season," said Amanda.

"Another *if*," said Callahan.

"But you said you heard rifle fire," said Amanda.

"It sounded like it," said Callahan, "but that doesn't mean someone was hunting. Could have just been target practice."

"So, you think the drone and rifle fire together on Bland's property were an innocent coincidence?" The sarcasm in Amanda's voice was obvious.

"Still too many *ifs* for me to think anything else right now. Let's start eliminating some of them. I want you to go back out to Bland's. Tell him you suspect someone is hunting on his property, and, if it's him, you want to make sure he has the appropriate hunting licenses. If it's not him, then ask if he has given anyone permission to hunt on his property and, if so, who? If he hasn't, then someone is trespassing; and we need to know about it," said Callahan.

"And if he still won't talk to me?" Amanda cocked her head and held her hands out in front of her, palms up, in a silent *what then?*

"Let's see how persuasive you can be," responded Callahan.

*   *   *

As Amanda approached the bunker, she drove slowly, scanning the sky above and beyond it for any drones. She only stopped her search when she parked the cruiser and adjusted the rearview mirror to check her hair. She wanted to look as professional as possible and had even stopped by her apartment to change into a fresh uniform before heading to Bland's. She was overdoing it, she knew, but the change of clothes made her feel more confident; and, after her last run-in with Bland, she needed all the confidence she could muster. Her nod to vanity had been to have the uniform slightly tailored so as not to totally hide her figure. It was enough to turn the phrase *There's something about a man in uniform* completely on its head, and she knew it.

When she felt composed, Amanda got out of the cruiser and walked to the entry door of the bunker. She was halfway there when the door opened.

"Good morning, Deputy Gillespie. Please come in," said Bland, smiling. He turned and stepped back into the bunker, waving over his shoulder for Amanda to follow. He walked down six semicircular stairs that expanded onto the floor of a massive living room, flanked on the left by a glimmering indoor swimming pool. As she followed Bland, Amanda caught the lingering scent of his cologne and was instantly transported to a place both exotic and earthily pleasurable. She'd never smelt anything like it before. The noise of the door shutting automatically behind her brought her back to reality. When she focused back on Bland, he was gesturing toward someone else in the room, standing off to his side and behind him. Amanda directed her attention to a tall man in his mid-thirties, bronze-skinned and handsome with a trimmed black beard. Like Bland, he was casually dressed in jeans and a polo shirt. Unlike Bland who wore flip flops, he sported expensive tan, soft-leather loafers.

"This is Abdullah bin Ra—"

"No need for formalities, just call me Abe," said Abdullah, cutting short Bland's introduction.

"Abe is being modest. He is here from Dubai and is Emirati royalty," continued Bland.

Amanda turned and looked at Bland quizzically.

"A prince," he said.

"Oh," said Amanda and, despite herself, sounded like a little girl opening a birthday present. She blushed in embarrassment.

"Please don't be impressed," said Abdullah. His words flowed with a smooth enunciation, but his sentence ended in a slight clip.

"There are many princes in the United Arab Emirates, and I am a very minor one."

"Abe and I go way back." Bland gave a conspiratorial wink to Abdullah. "We were roommates at Harvard." When Amanda responded with a wan smile, Bland abandoned his casual tone and became more formal. "Please, won't you sit down?" he said.

Amanda looked around for a seat and took in the room for the first time. The floor was polished stone of some kind. In the center, a large thick plate of cut glass sat atop a low sculpted marble slab of intertwined writhing bodies. Amanda found it both elegant and disturbing. Steel-framed leather furniture surrounded this center piece. Long thin windows stretched along the tops of the walls separating them from the ceiling and giving the impression that the roof of the bunker floated above the room. Below the windows, framed modern art decorated the four walls.

"Perhaps here," said Abdullah, pointing to a chair by a white leather couch.

Amanda walked to the chair and sat down. As she did, Abdullah sat down on the side of the couch nearest to Amanda. Bland took a chair across the table from the two of them.

"We're investigating the death of a girl found on the beach—Susan Gibbons," said Amanda.

"I've read about the death in your local paper. Tragic," said Bland.

"Yes," said Amanda. "So far, it appears that she was caught by the propellers of a large boat. We suspect that she either fell overboard or was swimming or diving when it happened."

"And you are telling me this because. . ." said Bland.

"Because you have a large yacht that was on the lake when and where she died," responded Amanda.

"I see. You're not suggesting foul play, are you? Abe is a Harvard law grad. Should I ask him to represent me?" Bland flashed a sly smile.

"No. Of course not. I mean, what we're doing now is eliminating possibilities. We want to know if Susan Gibbons was a guest on your yacht at any time, and if you or your crew suspected your yacht may have hit something in the water recently."

"I have no idea who Susan Gibbons is or was and can tell you that she was never on my yacht. I have no knowledge of the yacht hitting anything. However, if my word is not good enough for you, then, if he has no objections, you may question Abe. He has been my constant guest on the yacht since it set sail on the lake this summer." Bland eyed Abdullah and shrugged as if asking, *Any problem?*

Abdullah took the cue. "It would be a pleasure, but I can assure you now that Ms. Gibbons was never on the yacht when I was on board, and our sail, so far, has been perfectly smooth with no notable events at all." Abdullah grinned, cocked his head toward Bland, and then lowered his voice to a whisper. "With apologies to my host, but it has been rather boring," he said to Amanda.

"If you're still not satisfied, you're free to interview my crew and captain," said Bland. "You're even welcome to review the yacht's log and manifest. I want to be of whatever help I can. I live on this island too, you know."

"Thank you. Can we board your yacht tomorrow to interview the crew?" asked Amanda.

"Three of the crew stay here at the bunker when the yacht is docked: the chef and two deck hands. The captain and the rest of the crew stay on board. I will make everyone available at your convenience," said Bland.

Amanda stood up. When she did, so did Abdullah. Bland stayed seated. "One more thing," she said. "A drone was seen over your property the other day. Is it yours?"

"Is flying a drone illegal here?" asked Bland.

"Only if it's being used to hunt or harass hunters," said Amanda.

"Well then, the drone is mine, and it is used for security surveillance. I don't hunt, and no one hunts on my land," said Bland.

"Rifle fire was heard coming from your property the other day," said Amanda.

"That would've been me. I try to keep proficient in several weapons and have a firing range on my property. I don't shoot at anything but paper targets." Bland eased himself out of the chair. "I'll show you out," he said.

"Allow me," said Abdullah, and stepped quickly to Amanda's side. "A pity. Your stay has been too brief," he added as he escorted her to the door.

Amanda was not sure how to respond, so said nothing.

When they got to the door, Abdullah opened it; and, as Amanda was about to leave the bunker, he said, "There are many beautiful women in my emirate, but permit me to say that your beauty would put them to shame."

Chapter 7

JULIE SCOOTED HER CHAIR away from the filing cabinet, wheeled it over to her desk, and answered the station's non-emergency phone number with her standard salutation, "Sheriff's office, how may I help you?"

"Hi, Julie. This is Stephanie over at the school."

"Hi, Steph. How are you this morning?"

"Good, good. I don't have much time. I'm on a quick break, but I wanted to let you and Matt know that there is someone here at the school asking the principal questions about Susan. He came to my desk wanting to see the principal. I, of course, wanted to know why? As secretary of the school, I can't just let anyone in for any reason. The kids must be protected. You can't be too careful these days. He said he was here to inquire about Susan's death. I called the principal out, and the guy showed him some sort of ID; and the principal invited him into his office and closed the door. That's all I know except I took a picture of the license plate of the car he parked in the school lot. I can text it to you. Also, he's a man of color." This last sentence was whispered.

Julie rolled her eyes. Stephanie Rankin was the town gossip. Totally incorrigible in Julie's opinion. She wondered how she kept her job as the school's secretary with all the drama that swirled around the students, parents, and staff that had to be kept confidential: cheating, bullying, domestic violence, rumors of affairs, infighting, backbiting, jealousies—even an occasional theft of school supplies or petty cash. The list was endless, yet somehow Stephanie survived. Probably because of the skinny she had on everybody, thought Julie.

"Thank you, Steph, but that won't be necessary. I'm sure he will come and see Matt soon," said Julie.

"Well, just in case he doesn't, I'll text you the license plate number anyway; and if I find out who he is, I'll call you. Have to run now. Bye."

Julie's personal smart phone dinged with the text seconds later.

*   *   *

Callahan glanced up at the telephone message slip clipped to the cruiser's sun visor and then back at the license plate of the car in front of him. The number Julie had written on the slip matched the midnight blue Hyundai Elantra that had strictly followed the speed limit for the last two miles. Callahan turned on the cruiser's siren and light bar. The Hyundai pulled over to the shoulder of the road and stopped. Callahan rolled to a stop behind it. He immediately stepped out of the cruiser and walked over to the driver's side of the car, not bothering to run the plate through the cruiser's computer first.

The driver lowered his window, and before the glass had disappeared into the door, Callahan saw the startled look on his face. The flesh-colored plastic mask that covered the left side of Callahan's face triggered a confused surprise in those who saw him for the first time. Revulsion shoved aside surprise in those who spotted the purple mounds of flesh protruding under the edges of the mask and snaking down his neck. Acid thrown from a bottle had burned away half his face and left wounds that would never fully heal.

The driver looked away, and in the few seconds it took him to look back at Callahan, he had recovered his composure. "What's going on Sheriff? I've broken no laws. I wasn't speeding, the car's license and registration are current, and I know for a fact my turn signals and brake lights work," he said.

"I agree," said Callahan.

"Then what is this, a case of DWB?"

"You mean *Driving While Black*," stated Callahan.

"You got it right," said the driver.

Callahan smiled. "No, it is not. It's simply a case of curiosity," said Callahan.

"How so?" asked the driver.

"As to why someone would be interested in a death in my jurisdiction—a death my office is investigating—and not come to see me about it first," said Callahan.

The driver said nothing.

"I see. Then this is a case of DOS," said Callahan.

"DOS?" Now it was the driver's turn to query Callahan about an acronym.

"*Distrust of Sheriffs*," answered Callahan.

The driver laughed and shook his head. "My name's Miles Jackson, and I'm a federal marshal. I saw a diner just down the road. Can I buy you a cup of coffee? Maybe we can help each other," he said.

*   *   *

The exchange of pleasantries at the diner was at first perfunctory: a handshake, an introduction with a plea to call each other by their first names, a description of the delights of the diner by Callahan, and a nod to the mildness of the weather. But soon they each recognized in the other's demeanor a common background—they had both been police detectives. That broke the ice.

"So how long were you with the Detroit police, Miles?" asked Callahan.

"Five years. And you with the Chicago Police Department?"

"Fifteen," answered Callahan.

"So now you're a sheriff."

"Yes—long story, but it involved this." Callahan tapped the plastic prosthetic mask hiding the acid burns that disfigured the left side of his face. "And how about you?"

The waitress came by with a pot of coffee and nodded at the two of them. Miles raised his cup for a refill. When she left, he said, "My story's not so long. The US Marshals Service was looking for diversity. The Service wanted to recruit me. I said yes. Glad I did. I'm happy where I am now," answered Jackson.

"So, why's the US Marshals Service interested in Susan Gibbons?" asked Callahan.

"Her name isn't Susan Gibbons, and I suspect that most of what you know about her isn't true."

Callahan leaned forward and placed his elbows on the Formica table. "This is getting interesting. Please continue," he said.

"She was in the Witness Security Program. We gave her a deep cover identity and put her on this island because we thought she would never be discovered here. We may have been wrong."

Callahan slouched back into the seat of the booth. "Why was she in the program?" he asked.

"Unfortunately, the answer begins for her as an all too familiar story. She went to Thailand to teach English right out of college. She was young and beautiful but naïve. She was targeted, seduced, shackled by drugs, and then imprisoned in the high-priced sex trade in human trafficking. But then her story changes. She got smart fast and saw an opportunity when one of the kingpins took a shine to her. She eventually gained his confidence and used him to work her way up in the trade, ultimately helping to run its US connections. Then she escaped. But she'd learned too much. She knew they'd eventually find her, so she came to us for protection. She proved to be a gold mine of information, and we were using her to bring down the organization here in the US"

"You think they found her?" said Callahan.

"Could be. That's what I'm here to find out," said Jackson.

Chapter 8

A MANDA WAS TRANSCRIBING HER notes from the interview with Bland for the Gibbons file and wondered how much of her impressions she should include with the facts. Almost from the beginning, the atmosphere in the bunker made her uncomfortable. It was not the physical surroundings, but the atmosphere created by what she saw as a sly, confidential joke between Bland and Abdullah that made her feel both excluded and the joke's object. It was also the way Bland had introduced Abdullah to her, like a senior would introduce a freshman girl at a college frat party, expecting giddy adulation. And Abdullah's play on that introduction, especially his last remarks to her as she was leaving the bunker. Were they treating her like that because of her age, the fact that she was female, a contempt of her position as a mere deputy in Podunk, or was it all her imagination? And somehow Remy's crude remark about Susan Gibbons' sexual proclivities was intertwined in all of this. For a reason she did not quite understand, she found it abusive; and she was now sorry she had not confronted Remy about it. She was still struggling with these thoughts when Callahan entered the station and walked over to her desk.

"You can stop looking into the background of Susan Gibbons because the one you're going to find doesn't exist," he said.

Amanda looked up, both surprised by his sudden presence and puzzled by his out-of-the-blue statement. "What does that even mean?" she stammered.

Callahan took a deep breath. "Just had coffee with the mystery man from the school. He's a federal marshal investigating the death of Susan Gibbons, who isn't Susan Gibbons but a witness under a false identity in the Witness Security Program, giving the government evidence against a human trafficking outfit. Or, at least, she was a witness."

It took a moment for Amanda to take this in until the consequences of it hit her. "Damn. That must mean that most of what I've found out about her background is useless," she said.

"Yep, pretty much. Unless you found out she was in the Witness Security Program," said Callahan.

Amanda shook her head. "Did not do that," she sighed.

"I guess that's proof the program works," teased Callahan.

"What now?" asked Amanda.

"Now we work with Miles Jackson of the US Marshals Service," said Callahan. "Seems like a nice guy," he added.

Callahan was driving along the lower stretch of road that edged the west side of the island. The dust had been tamped down by the spray of a water truck, and the dirt road glistened in scattered pools of reflected sunlight. The summer had been unusually dry, and besides the nuisance of thick plumes of dust from traffic on the web of dirt roads throughout the island, the threat of forest fires was at its height. He was looking for campsites outside designated camping areas, a common cause of fires on the island.

The roadway darkened as Callahan plunged into a long tunnel of trees whose branches arched over the road, and he almost didn't see the man standing in the middle of the road ahead waving his arms in a signal to stop. Callahan jammed on the brakes and skidded the cruiser onto the shoulder. He powered down the window and shouted, "What the hell are you doing, Sully? Are you trying to get yourself killed?"

Jack Sullivan jogged over to the cruiser and lowered his head to face Callahan through the opened window. The smell of tobacco and stale sweat wafted into the cruiser.

"Sorry about that, Sheriff. But I didn't want you to scoot by me. I was just about to call into the station. You've got to see this." Sullivan opened the door to the cruiser and slid into the back seat. "Turn left up the road where it intersects with McCauley's Way. It's just a short jaunt on from there."

Callahan steered the cruiser back onto the road. "What's going on Sully?" he asked.

"Not sure, but it's trouble of some kind, and it looks like someone's going to get hurt." Sullivan hunched forward. "Turn here," he said, and then pointed over Callahan's shoulder through the windshield. "There. Right there," he said.

Ahead, the county water truck was stopped; and around it was a crowd of people. Even from a distance Callahan could tell the crowd had not assembled out of curiosity or for welcome or assistance. It was angry. He could hear the muffled bursts of shouts and see the agitated gesticulations of individuals. Callahan drove the cruiser nearer the assembled mass of people and then stopped and got out. Several members of the crowd turned and walked towards him. He recognized a couple of them. They had homes along McCauley's Way. He also saw the driver of the water truck lean out the window towards him and raise his arms in a gesture of helplessness.

"What's going on here?" said Callahan.

Everyone started to talk at once until a tall man at the front raised his hand to silence the group. "Good morning, Sheriff. What this is is a protest. And a serious one. The poisoning of our well water has got to stop."

"That's right," said a woman just behind the tall man. "I've got kids, and I'm going to make damn sure they're safe."

"That truck doesn't move another inch forward unless it's over my dead body," said another woman in the group.

"I don't get it," said Callahan. "What's a water truck got to do with poisoning your well water?"

The tall man spoke again. "These water trucks spray road brine, which is waste water from oil extraction wells on the mainland. The county gets it free from the oil companies. It's contaminated, poison actually, and it's seeping into our drinking water."

More people from the crowd began to gather around Callahan and started shouting at him.

"You've got to help us, Sheriff."

"Yeah, arrest these bastards."

"This is assault. They're killing us."

Callahan shouldered his way past the group and then pushed through the crowd to the driver's side of the truck. He stepped on the running board and pulled himself toward the window where the driver stared down at him. "If I move this crowd back, will you turn this thing around and head back into town?" he said.

38 —

"Sure thing, Sheriff. I just want to get out of here."

Callahan stepped down and turned toward the crowd. "Okay, everyone. You've had your say and made your point. This truck is leaving. Go home and take this up with the county commissioner."

"We tried that, and it didn't work," someone yelled.

"This truck is done for the day. No more spraying. It's leaving. Now move back," said Callanan. He signaled for the driver to start backing up.

As the truck began to move, Callahan walked behind it, separating the crowd. When the truck passed through the crowd, Callahan ran to the cruiser, jumped behind the wheel, and escorted the truck to the intersection where it backed onto the road and sped away. So did Callahan.

Chapter 9

"HOW VALID IS EVERYONE'S concern over the water trucks?" Callahan stood at the window of Collin O'Donnell's office, looking out over the bay and drinking a cup of coffee. The office had a much different feel—open and inviting—now that O'Donnell had taken it over from Tom Breslin along with Breslin's job as head of the board of commissioners. Thanks to dogged detective work by Callahan and Amanda, Breslin was spending the rest of his life in prison for murder.

O'Donnell sat at his desk and began typing on his computer as he spoke. "First of all, not everyone is concerned about the water trucks. It's just a few rabid summer residents and the usual local trouble makers. Second, they're technically not water trucks. They spray road brine or waste water from oil wells on the mainland. The oil companies give it to us. It saves them money because they can dispose of it at little or no cost, and it saves this county tens of thousands of dollars a year. Do you have any idea how many miles of dirt road we have on this island?"

Callahan shrugged, and O'Donnell stopped typing.

"A hell of a lot," continued O'Donnell. "Plus, road brine works much better in tamping down dust on dirt roads than pure water, which doesn't work at all, or even water mixed with rock salt."

"Then why the riot yesterday?" asked Callahan.

O'Donnell turned to Callahan with an expression that said, *Give me a break.*

"Okay, so it wasn't exactly a riot. Then what's going on?" asked Callahan.

O'Donnell pointed to the screen of his laptop. "Take a look. Apparently, the demonstration was staged. According to today's online edition of the *Nicolet Ledger,* whose reporter was there, residents intend to stop all spraying on the island and have planned human roadblocks of the water trucks in the future."

Callahan leaned over O'Donnell's shoulder and peered at the article. When he straightened up, O'Donnell slammed shut the laptop's screen and spun his chair around to face Callahan. "A few of the summer residents have been spreading the rumor that the spray is toxic and seeping into their well water. We've had some of the wells tested and there's no problem," he said.

"Is the spray toxic?" asked Callahan.

O'Donnell hesitated a moment before answering. "It does contain contaminants. Yes."

"How bad are they?" pressed Callahan.

The question was not welcome. O'Donnell's cherubic face slackened and lost its ruddiness. "It depends on whose report you read," he said.

Callahan suspected O'Donnell had read all the reports and knew the consensus. "Collin, people bike and walk on those roads and breathe in the dust," said Callahan.

"I know," said O'Donnell.

Chapter 10

A MANDA WATCHED AS THE man wended his way between the sprawled mats of bearberry that covered the interdunes along Pebble Bay. He progressed slowly with the flatfooted stumble of all who traversed the soft sands of the island's western dunes. Amanda called and waved, and the man looked up and waved back. He turned and headed her way. Franklin Hollander had called Julie at the station and insisted that she dispatch Amanda to the bay immediately as there'd be something there that would interest her professionally. Something important, he'd said. Amanda assumed it had to do with protecting the ecology of the bay. Hollander had appointed himself a one-man guardian of the flora and fauna, patrolling the shore and reporting every transgression to the sanctity of the protected species on the bay. He wanted access to the bay restricted because he was convinced that the Piping Plover was nesting there again and that the Pitcher's Thistle was being trampled into extinction.

When Hollander reached her, he was slightly winded and paused a moment to catch his breath. "You've seen it then, have you?" he said in an exhaled breath.

"I don't think so, Frank. What do you mean?" said Amanda.

"There," he said, sweeping his arm around behind him and pointing north inside the bay. "How could you miss it?"

Amanda followed the direction of his arm until she saw it. He was right. The barge was huge and stacked high with pipes and unassembled scaffolding. Its closeness to the shore made it blend in with the trees of the back dunes. Amanda guessed that this was why she hadn't noticed it at first.

"Listen," Hollander said and held a finger to his lips.

Amanda concentrated, but all she could hear was the wash of the waves and the shrill gulping of distant gulls. Then she felt it more than heard it. A dull throbbing that quickly became a violent slapping as a helicopter rounded the point of the bay and hovered over the barge. As if drawn by a pencil, a line lowered from the belly of the copter. When it reached the scaffolding, the barge's deck began to quiver with activity, and Amanda could hear muffled shouts and the clank of metal from across the water.

"This has been going on for a couple of days now. Don't know for sure, but my guess is the stuff on the barge is being dropped onto Tom Egan's property. Tom won't say, but, even before the barge arrived, the talk around the bar at O'Malley's was that he's going to be rich—very rich."

Chapter 11

✪✪

T HE BEECHCRAFT QUEEN AIR floated down from the sky until it touched the runway like a feather settling on a pillow and then taxied to the terminal. The rotations of its twin props slowed and then simultaneously jolted to a halt as the airstair passenger door was lowered. Nick Randolph was the first to deplane. Amanda ran out on the tarmac to meet him. They gave each other a quick kiss as they walked back to the terminal.

She and Nick had been dating for a year, but their days together totaled only a few weeks, a sum that for her seemed like a string of just a few short hours. It wasn't enough. Nick was finishing his PhD at the university in Ann Arbor and working in the university's Center for the Study of Domestic Terrorism. She was now entrenched in the job she had always yearned for since starting high school, deputy sheriff of Nicolet County. Their relationship strained under the pull of distance, and she worried.

"It seems like forever since I've seen you," said Amanda.

"It's only been a week," said Nick.

"That's forever," said Amanda.

Nick laughed and then looked serious. "There's no good time to tell you this so I might as well do it now," he said.

"What?" asked Amanda, getting serious herself.

"We're going to have to stop meeting like this," he said.

Amanda stopped walking and pulled on his arm to stop him too. "What do you mean?" she asked.

"Flying here and then back to the mainland almost every weekend is getting very expensive. Frankly, I can't afford it," Nick answered. "And you can't leave the island most weekends because of your job."

As the other passengers swept around them to get to their luggage, Amanda stared at Nick with an unmistakable look of panic on her face. "Are you saying we can't see each other as much?" she stammered.

Nick lowered his head and stared at the ground. "No, that's not what I'm saying," he answered.

"Then are you saying we can't see each other at all?" she nearly screamed.

Nick looked back up and then reached out and gently held Amanda's face in his hands. Amanda's body stiffened. She knew that this relationship was too good to be true, that it wouldn't last. His gesture wasn't of affection but was a prelude to a big fat letdown, a signal she should not freak out with the bad news. She just knew it.

"What I'm trying to say is that it's time I moved to the island."

Amanda stood in front of Nick, stunned. Then she jumped and threw her arms around his neck, squeezing him until he almost choked.

When she stepped back, her elation instantly turned to apprehension again, and the questions came tumbling over one another.

"When? Are you sure about this? What about your job? What about finishing your PhD? Are you really sure this is what you want?"

"Yes, I'm sure, and I've worked everything out. The University of Michigan's biological and environmental station on the island is expanding and needs a computer expert to handle its data. I applied for a transfer from the university's Center for the Study of Domestic Terrorism and was accepted. I didn't want to tell you until it was a done deal. Apparently, the competition was stiff. I start next week. And I've finished all the coursework for my doctorate. All I have to do now is write my dissertation. I can do that here on the island with an occasional trip to the mainland."

Amanda took Nick's hand and escorted him into the terminal. She didn't say anything until he'd gotten his bag and backpack. Then she said, not to him, but more to herself, "This is a surprise."

"I'm sorry," he said. "I thought you'd be happy about it."

"I am. Beyond happy even, ecstatic. It's just that . . ."

"What?"

"Where will you live?"

"I thought that maybe you and I could . . . you know . . ."

"This is a small island. People talk, and my parents live here." Amanda's words sounded more like a plea than a statement.

Nick nodded. "Fair enough," he said.

* * *

Amanda and Nick arrived at the ferry dock in time to watch a nervous sales representative accompany two forklifts as they wheeled the brand new twenty-seven-foot Boston Whaler Vigilant on its pallet to the boat crane at the end of the pier. Callahan and O'Donnell were at the front of a small group of curious locals and ferry workers following the progress.

"She's a real beauty," said Callahan when Amanda and Nick had made their way to the group. Callahan nodded to Nick in greeting. The boat was beautiful, featuring a forward pilot house with a Whelen light bar and siren and a gleaming white hull emblazoned with the county crest trailed by the designation *Sheriff* sandwiched between bold trim markings. Her mission was unmistakable. Then he said to Amanda, "When they get her in the water, we're to take her to her berth in the marina the long way 'round. That will be her shakedown cruise and our introduction to the operation of her many features, all customized to her law enforcement duties. Her sales representative will be our instructor."

"She and her customized features, including those two twin Yamaha engines, didn't come cheap. She cost the county a pretty penny, so don't break her," said O'Donnell.

"No worries. According to the sales rep she's supposed to have an unsinkable hull," said Callahan. O'Donnell didn't look convinced.

Neither did Amanda. "Do you think that's true?" she whispered to Callahan.

"Let's hope we don't have to find out," he said as the crane settled the boat onto the water. Bobbing gently next to the pier, she looked very proud to be there, he thought.

Chapter 12

CALLAHAN, JULIE, AND MAX sat on a bluff above the beach and watched the sun set over the lake. No two sunsets were ever the same, and tonight a band of robin's egg blue stretched across the horizon and flared into a scarlet flame that turned the clouds crimson. It lasted only seconds before it disappeared. Since buying the house, this had become their tradition before settling in for the evening. Even the dog participated and somehow knew to be still and quiet until the show was over. Then it made a mad dash up the path to the house and spun in frantic circles at the door until Julie let it in for its nightly peanut butter dog biscuit.

As Max set up the checkerboard on the living room coffee table, Julie and Callahan began cleaning up the after-dinner clutter in the kitchen.

"Have you heard about anything unusual happening over at Tom Egan's place?" asked Callahan.

"I don't think so. What do you mean?" said Julie.

"Amanda told me she saw a helicopter offloading equipment from a barge in Pebble Bay. Frank Hollander told her that he thought the load was being delivered to Egan's property. She said that was all he knew about it."

"Hmm. I haven't heard anything about Egan, but I did pick up chatter on the station's radio scanner over the past couple of days. It sounded like the air to ground communications from the pilots of Island Air we sometimes pick up so I didn't think much of it, except that the pilot identified himself with a callsign that I didn't recognize. Also, the pilot gave his distance and direction from Pebble Bay. Oh, and he said something about delivering a passenger from Beacon or Beaumont or something like that. That's why I thought it might be a flight from Island Air. Could that have been the helicopter?"

"Don't know and not sure if I should even look into it. Doesn't appear any laws were broken, and no one's complained. It just seems curious that nobody knows anything about it, including O'Donnell who constantly has his ear to the ground for anything that's happening in the county. If you hear any more of that chatter though, let me know."

Max appeared at the kitchen door and stood there expectantly. "Okay, buddy. Is the checkerboard all ready to go?" said Callahan.

Max nodded.

"Can you wait to start the game for one more minute?" asked Julie.

Max shook his head.

"Then let the game begin. I guess your mother will have to finish in here by her lonesome," said Callahan, tossing a dishtowel on the sink counter and smiling at Julie. "I do love checkers," he added as he left the kitchen with Max.

Chapter 13

❧

THE BOAT SKIPPED OVER the light chop at thirty-five knots, the prow rising just inches above crests of small waves before dipping and smacking the water to rise again. This was all it took for Callahan.

"Can't you go any faster?" Callahan shouted back to Amanda over the roar of the engines as he held tight to the starboard bow rail with both hands.

Amanda nudged the throttle forward an inch, and the boat sped ahead. Callahan leaned slightly over the rail and raised one arm, and Amanda eased back the throttle until the boat slowed to a sturdy glide. "Is it time to chum for carp again?" she said.

"Not funny," he said and promptly threw up over the side of the boat.

It had started with a slight headache. Then came the clammy feeling to his skin, followed by a cold sweat and nausea, and ending with a sudden bout of projectile vomiting.

"I can't believe this is happening," said Callahan. "I never get seasick."

"That's a myth. Everyone gets seasick sooner or later," said Amanda.

"Not comforting," said Callahan.

"Do you want to turn back?"

"No. We've come too far. We're almost to the bay. Just give me a second."

Amanda waited until Callahan raised his arm again. "Let's get this over fast," he said. She pushed the throttle forward, and the boat flew toward the bay with Callahan desperately hanging on.

As they rounded the point, the deck barge came into view; and Amanda dropped the engines' rpms to almost zero and coasted the boat to the barge's side. Its steel hull was massive with a deck that rested high above the waterline. Amanda had to crane her head back to see the large man in a hard hat, a soiled t-shirt, and ripped jeans looking down at her.

"Is there a problem, Sheriff?" he yelled.

Amanda turned to Callahan who was retching over the rail and thought it best that she answer his question.

"No problem," said Amanda. "We were on patrol and saw your barge. We're just curious. What are you doing here?"

"Just delivering some equipment to the island. We're almost finished. We'll be out of here before noon. Our towboat is on the way from the mainland."

"What kind of equipment is it, and what's it for?" asked Amanda.

"Can't answer either question, because I don't know. We weren't told." The large man looked over his shoulder and nodded. "If all's good, I've got to get back to work," he said.

"Wait," said Callahan rallying enough to speak. "Where's that stuff going to on the island?"

The large man looked over his shoulder again and appeared to be listening to someone. Then he turned back to Callahan. "If you have more questions, call the owner of the barge. Maybe he can help you. We work for Superior Tow and Salvage," he said and then vanished as a helicopter appeared over the trees along the shore and headed toward the barge. It was yellow with the letters *STS* stenciled along the fuselage.

* * *

Callahan and Amanda made it back to the marina in time for Callahan to drive home, shower, change clothes, and meet Jackson at the cottage rented by Susan Gibbons. He still felt a bit unsteady, but the shower and solid ground had diminished the worst of his symptoms. Although Susan's death hadn't been declared a homicide and the cottage wasn't a crime scene, Callahan had prevailed upon the cottage's owner to delay advertising it for rent and allow him and Jackson to go through it. The owner was to meet Callahan there. Callahan and Jackson arrived separately but at almost the same time. The owner sat in a neon-blue plastic Adirondack chair on the cottage's deck and stood when they got out of their vehicles.

"Hi, Sheriff," he said. "You're right on time."

"Hi, Ben. This is good of you. Thanks, I appreciate it," said Callahan and then turned to introduce Jackson. "Ben, this is Miles Jackson, he is—"

"—here representing the family," said Jackson, completing the sentence before Callahan could.

Callahan smiled to himself as he noted that Jackson wasn't being entirely dishonest. "Miles, this is Ben McIntyre. He owns this property," he said, finishing the introduction.

McIntyre glanced quizzically at Callahan as he shook hands with Jackson. "I was wondering when the family was going to collect the belongings," he said to Jackson. "I called the number she provided on the rental form and was told that the family would be contacted."

"They have been, and arrangements are being made to remove Miss Gibbons' property," said Jackson. "You'll be notified soon of a date."

"Great," said the owner. He opened the front door and started to enter.

Callahan laid a hand on the owner's shoulder. "Do you mind waiting outside, Ben?" The way Callahan asked and the weight of his hand on the owner's shoulder made only one answer appropriate.

The owner stepped back and watched Jackson closely as he entered the cottage. Then he looked at Callahan for assurance. Callahan's face remained impassive. "Okay, sure, no problem. I'll be here on the deck," he said.

✳　✳　✳

Callahan shut the door and surveyed the interior of the cottage. It was tiny: two rooms with an open loft under a peaked ceiling. Below the loft was the bedroom with the rest of the first floor serving as the kitchen, living room, dining room, and a small bathroom with shower. Yet, somehow Susan had decorated the interior to make it look spacious. A creative placement of a few items of furniture and accessories divided the lower level into inviting and cozy spaces. Susan had transformed the loft with its skylight into an art studio and spare bedroom containing an easel and futon. A curtain of hanging beads gave a touch of privacy.

"This doesn't look like it will take long," said Jackson. "Where should we work first?"

"Let's start with the bedroom," said Callahan.

Both he and Jackson put on latex gloves, and Jackson opened the bedroom door. He didn't enter but just stood in the doorway. Callahan peered over Jackson's shoulder. The miniscule bedroom was barely big enough for the bed, night stand, built-out closet, and dresser that it contained. It was not big enough for two large men.

"I'll take the loft," said Callahan.

"Good idea," said Jackson.

The first thing Callahan noticed about the loft was the feel of it, its atmosphere. Unlike the downstairs of the cottage, which had a comfortable and welcoming lure, this space felt intimate to the point of exclusion. It seemed unmistakably an extension of Susan herself, not meant for anyone else. Callahan sensed that it was here that Susan lived. She merely occupied the rest of the cottage, and he felt like an intruder invading a sanctuary.

The loft served as a studio, and paintings of different island wild flowers festooned the room. All were remarkable in color and composition; all initially compelling. But framed painting of trilliums that leaned against the wall on the floor especially intrigued Callahan, and he picked it up and inspected it carefully. Susan had signed it, and it was as beautiful as all the others but disturbing in a way Callahan couldn't quite pin down. The flowers clustered and formed a spill of muted white against the profusion of greens that almost overwhelmed them. The cluster occupied only a small segment of the painting yet was dominant. Callahan tried to discern why. Then he *saw* what he had only casually observed before. One trillium at the edge of the floral spill stretched from the sandy soil, its stem tilted toward the sunlit far corner of the painting. Two of its petals were raised while one seemed to droop as if shrinking from the light. Where the petals joined was a small orb of yellow so bright that it served to dull the sunlight and irresistibly draw the eye of the observer to the flower. As he studied the flower, faint images came into view.

The two raised petals formed hands, their fingers coiled as if clutching at something; and below them, in the sand at the base of the stem swirled the unmistakable curls of vanished snakes. Before he put the picture down, he instinctively turned it around to inspect the back. In one corner, a thin folded rectangle of paper was taped to the side of the frame. The paper was the same color as the frame and barely visible. Callahan peeled back the tape and removed the rectangle. He set the picture on the futon and gently unfolded the paper. Then he carefully inspected the canvases and frames of all the other paintings in the room.

"Miles, I think I've found something," he called.

Jackson stood outside the bedroom below the loft, looking up at Callahan. "Me too," he said.

Chapter 14

❧

"**W**HAT HAVE YOU GOT?" said Jackson when he reached the top of the loft stairs.

"Not sure, but I found this taped to the back of that painting." Callahan nodded at the painting on the futon and handed the paper to Jackson.

Jackson took the paper and examined it. He shrugged and handed it back to Callahan. "Could be a name," said Jackson. "*Rahu*. It doesn't mean anything to me. Maybe she taped it to the painting to identify who she wanted to receive the painting or who commissioned or bought it. Did you check to see if any of the other paintings had names taped to them?"

"Yes," said Callahan. "None of the others had anything taped to them or any markings of any kind on the back. This was the only one."

"Hmm. It's probably nothing," said Jackson. "Let's check the rest of the house." He started down the stairs.

"Wait," said Callahan. "You said you found something. What is it?"

"It's a receipt," said Jackson continuing down the stairs. Callahan followed. "I took a picture of it and left it on her night stand. Found it under her bed. It probably fell out of her purse and wound up there. It's from some business in Grand Rapids. Can't tell what kind from the name," said Jackson.

Callahan waited for Jackson to continue, but he didn't. Instead, Jackson stood at the foot of the stairs lost in thought. "And is it somehow significant?" asked Callahan.

Jackson snapped back into the present. "Could be. She wasn't supposed to travel any distance without telling us where she was going, why, and for how long. If she did go to Grand Rapids, we didn't know about it."

"How much is the receipt for?" asked Callahan.

"Three hundred and fifty dollars," answered Jackson.

"What's the name of the business?"

"*The Grotto.*"

"Get your phone out and Google it for Grand Rapids," said Callahan.

"Sometimes I wonder if I belong in the modern age," said Jackson and looked chagrined as he pulled his phone from his pocket and began tapping in the name on its browser. He peered at the screen for a moment and then said, "It's an art gallery and coffee house."

"Well, if she bought a painting there, it isn't here. All the paintings are in the loft, and all are signed by her," said Callahan.

"Maybe she sold one there," mused Jackson.

"Do you think it's worth following up?" said Callahan.

"This art thing was a part of her life she didn't tell us about. For that reason alone, it's probably worth a trip to Grand Rapids," said Jackson.

"Let's finish up here," said Callahan as he reaffixed the note to the back of the picture frame with the tape.

As they split up to search the first floor, Jackson said, "There's no computer in the bedroom, and I didn't find her cell phone in there either."

Chapter 15

FINN GALLAGHER LEANED OVER his desk and read the article again with relish. The *Ledger* had just published its first scoop in years. Although calling the article a scoop was a bit of a stretch since there were no other newspapers on the island. But that's how he chose to view it. The article was big news, and big news was a scoop. Especially since the *Ledger* had beaten social media to the punch—a rarity. Plus, the facts were critical to the islanders and tantalizing enough to generate public and media notice beyond the island. He had already gotten a call from *The Detroit Free Press* about the article. That meant an increase in circulation and more advertising sales for the financially strapped newspaper. As editor of the *Ledger,* he was a happy man.

Gallagher had uncovered the drilling himself. In retrospect, it had all been rather simple. He'd heard from Franklin Hollander about the barge in Pebble Bay. He'd gone there, taken pictures of the barge and its freight, emailed them each to a construction company, a bridge company, an oil company, and a crane-building company in Wisconsin. The responses were timely. The freight wasn't made up of parts for a bridge, scaffold, or crane, but component parts for a drilling rig. The next step he thought would be pro forma, merely calling Michigan's Department of Environmental Quality, the agency that issues permits for drilling, and asking who was drilling in Nicolet County and for what. It was all a matter of public record, or so he thought. But the Department's answer to his inquiry was a curt but emphatic, *No comment.* That's when he discovered that a little-known provision of Michigan's Natural Resources and Environmental Protection Act allowed for *all* information and data on certain types of drilling to be held confidential for ten years. And such information and data were even exempt from disclosure under the Freedom of Information Act. In short, Michigan permitted oil and mining companies to drill in secret. And it was happening on the island.

Per Hollander, a company was constructing the rig on Tom Egan's land, and Gallagher had called Egan to confirm the story. Egan had hung up on him and promptly taken an unseasonal trip to his winter condo in Florida where he became incommunicado. So, without any hard facts about the drilling, the article produced speculation, which quickly became rumor, which ramped up to fear mongering, until uttering the word *fracking* generated panic among the islanders. Concerned islanders planned a huge protest at Egan's property, and a network affiliated TV station from Traverse City was flying in a crew by helicopter to cover it. Life was good, thought Gallagher.

Chapter 16

A MANDA ARRIVED AT EGAN'S property well before the announced start of the protest, and already pickup trucks and SUVs lined both sides of the dirt road that paralleled the property's frontage. Two of the island's cafés had set up makeshift concession stands and were doing a brisk business in coffee, donuts, and bottled water. It wasn't long before the lines of vehicles stretched so far down the road in each direction that Amanda couldn't see the end of them. The crowd steadily swelled until it kicked up enough dust to generate a permanent haze over the area. Yet, the atmosphere felt more jovial than angry, and she enjoyed reading the placards people held aloft as they passed the TV camera: *Keep the holes off our island and with the asses where they belong; Don't frack with us; If there's nothing to hide then DON'T.* She particularly liked the poster depicting Nicolet Island as a hornet's nest with a swarm of furious hornets diving toward an oil rig being erected on the island.

"Are you here to quell the revolt?"

The question surprised Amanda, and she was startled to see Tony Bland standing next to her. He smiled, and she smiled back. "No, just keeping an eye on things. What about you? Why are you here?"

"Just came to add my small voice to the general din," he said.

"You're anti-drilling then?" said Amanda. She had not thought of Bland as being against drilling and was afraid the surprise had registered in her voice.

"Let's say that I'm willing to support any fracas that keeps the sheriff away from my property." Bland smiled again and added, "Does anyone know what's really happening here?"

Amanda shrugged.

"That's what I thought. Perhaps it's good you're here then."

"What do you mean?" asked Amanda.

Bland swept his hand across the crowd in front of them. "This free-floating mass antagonism can attach itself to the wrong appeal and become dangerous," he answered.

"Things look pretty tame to me," said Amanda.

"For now," said Bland.

"That sounds ominous," said Amanda.

"Then let's move on to a more pleasant matter. My friend was very taken with you the other day. He would like to see you again. My yacht will be here this weekend with some friends aboard, and I'm throwing a party for them. He'll be among them. I'd like you to join us."

"Thanks for the invitation, but tell your friend I'm in a relationship," said Amanda.

Bland didn't blink. "Not a problem. Bring him," he hesitated a second, "or her along. Be at the pier Saturday evening at 9:00 and a boat will be there to take the two of you to the yacht. My parties are not to be missed."

"That's nice, but my answer is still no."

"It's an open invitation. If you change your mind, I'll see you then."

Bland spread his arms, and Amanda, thinking he was inviting a hug, recoiled as he stepped past her, pretending to embrace the crowd before he waded into it.

Chapter 17

CALLAHAN AND JULIE SAT next to each other, sunk low in their beach chairs, and watched as Max searched for the right stones among the rocks jumbled along the beach. The dog, intent upon its own interests, darted from one shrub to the next but always just behind Max. This part of the island was not popular because of its muddy beach and shallow water, but they came often because they both loved it. The low vegetation over the wide stretch of the flats from the woods to the water reminded them of a Scottish moor, and the stones here were like no others on the island, flat, scoured by the wind and sand, and perfect for stacking. So perfect that visitors constructed cairns along the water's edge. Although man-made, the small precarious towers seemed an innate part of the landscape and gave it a numinous aura and its name—Mystic Point.

"What do you make of our island becoming the home of federally protected witnesses?" Callahan asked Julie. His question interrupted the comfortable silence between them.

"You mean the one we know of?" she said after a moment.
Callahan nodded.

"Well, I hadn't really thought about it, but I take it from your question that you're against it or at least have doubts about it," said Julie.

"I do have my doubts."

"Why?" asked Julie

As Callahan spoke, he stared out across the water as if thinking aloud. "I just don't like the possibilities. If Susan Gibbons' death wasn't an accident, then that could mean that someone on the island discovered her true identity and revealed it to whoever wanted her dead. And that could mean that someone on the island has a connection to the criminal syndicate she was a part of. Maybe even that person was ordered to kill her." Callahan turned to face Julie. "See what I mean?"

"Those are weighty speculations. No wonder you've been so quiet," said Julie.

"I'm only dealing with the possibilities," said Callahan.

Julie thought for a moment. "If that's the case, there's another possibility," she said.

"What is it?" asked Callahan.

"What if it wasn't someone on the island who revealed her identity?" Julie posited.

"What do you mean?"

"Well, who in the Witness Security Program had access to her file, and what do you really know about Jackson?"

Low clouds scudded above them, and whitecaps began to form in the shallow water off the point. "We'd better go. The weather's changing," said Callahan, abruptly ending their conversation. He stood up and grabbed the beach chair. He fumbled with folding it, and Julie could tell he was miffed. She guessed it was with himself. He hated overlooking anything.

"I'm only saying," she said.

Chapter 18

꩜

JACKSON TOOK THE EXIT ramp off Route 131 and followed Mt Vernon Avenue to its intersection with Fulton Street where he turned left and crossed the Grand River into downtown Grand Rapids. He drove east on Fulton for three blocks until his GPS announced that his destination was on the right. Thankfully, so was a parking space.

The Grotto turned out to be an upscale coffee shop and art gallery that dispensed more coffee than art. Jackson got in line and waited while excessively cheerful baristas prepared impossibly personalized caffeinated concoctions for their metro-chic customers. By the time it was his turn to order, he felt annoyed as hell. He asked for a cappuccino—whole milk with three sugars—to be delivered by the manager.

"Is there a problem?" asked his barista without once diminishing the wattage of her smile.

"No problem. Just interested in the work of one of your artists. Want to know more about her paintings is all."

"Oh, okay. If you'd like to find a table, I'll go get the manager. He should be able to help you. He handles the artwork. Give me your name, and we'll call you when your cappuccino's ready."

"It's Miles," said Jackson and sidestepped away from the register to make room for the next customer. At every table, someone sat typing on a laptop, craning over a tablet, or thumbing a text on a phone; and he had to wait until a woman, holding a phone to her ear, hurriedly left a table next to the wall. He had just sat down when the manager appeared.

"What can I do for you?" said a young man half Jackson's age with long hair twisted into a man bun at the back of his head.

"Susan Gibbons. You've sold some of her paintings here, I think. I'm interested in her work."

The manager sat down at the table and handed Jackson his coffee. "Are you an art dealer?"

Jackson took a sip and then answered. "No. Just a prospective buyer; a collector of sorts. A friend has one of her paintings and told me she exhibits and sells her work here. She apparently doesn't have a website to sell online. At least, I couldn't find one."

"I don't know about that, but she does send some paintings here occasionally. We sell them on consignment. She hasn't sent any new ones to us in a while, but there's one on the wall in our gallery now." The manager gestured toward another room to his left.

"Great. I'd like to look at it, but I may want to take it off the wall to examine it closely. Do you mind?" said Jackson.

The manager chuckled. "Not if you put it back. Or buy it," he added.

*   *   *

The painting was of wild flowers, and even to Jackson's untrained eye, it appeared to be a sophisticated work of art, not the usual amateur rendering hanging on most coffeehouse walls. He removed it from its hanger and inspected the front and back of the frame and canvas. Nothing was affixed anywhere on the painting. He hung it back on the wall and went looking for the manager. He found him behind the counter and signaled for his attention. The manager whispered something to the barista next to him and then came over to Jackson.

"You want to buy that painting?" he asked.

"I'd like to see more of her work. Could you tell me who bought her paintings recently? Maybe I could contact them about seeing the paintings they purchased," said Jackson.

"I can't help you there. It's odd, but she only had one purchaser, and he paid cash and never gave us his name. He bought several of her paintings though, usually the most expensive ones. She priced them high. He was always here when the new ones arrived, like he wanted to make sure no one else bought them. I haven't seen him in here for a while."

"What did he look like? Maybe I can catch him if he comes back," said Jackson.

"He was older than me but younger than you, and he was white. Dark hair. Long. You'd recognize him. He was tall or would be, but he walked kind of stooped, you know, bent over a little, like he was looking for something he dropped on the floor. Maybe he had problems with his back."

"Appreciate it," said Jackson and grabbed a napkin from the dispenser on the counter. He wrote his first name and telephone number on it and handed the napkin to the manager. "I'll keep an eye out for him, but if you see him before I do, will you give him my number?"

The manager took the napkin and nodded.

Jackson started to leave but then stopped. "By the way, your coffee's good here."

"Thanks," said the manager.

Chapter 19

AMANDA TRIED NOT TO let them bother her, but she couldn't chase Remy's words from her mind or quell the sick feeling in her gut when she thought of them—and she was thinking of them a lot. At first, she had berated herself for being overly sensitive, even prudish; but now felt that his offhanded callous remark about Susan Gibbons having had more pricks in her than a dive bar dart board was truly disgusting and diminishing to women. He needn't have described the evidence of her sexual activity in such an embarrassing and degrading way. Amanda had been offended, and she wanted Remy to know it. Her brooding had hardened into a resolve to confront him about the crassness and sexism he displayed in the morgue, and she was plotting ways to do it when he called her.

"You got a minute?" he asked.

"Yeah, sure," said Amanda.

"Good, because this might be important. Gibbons was found on the beach nude, and I had initially assumed that she had gone in the water that way. But she might have been wearing clothing, most likely a bathing suit that could have been torn off when she was lacerated by the prop blades of the boat that ran over her. So, I searched her wounds again for traces of fiber or cloth and found something else." Remy paused.

"What?" asked Amanda.

"There were cloth fibers, so she was wearing clothing; but there were also minute flecks and shards of plastic embedded in the wounds on her arms and chest."

"She was holding something?" asked Amanda.

"That was my conclusion too, and it must have been fairly large because the plastic is deep and distributed throughout her chest and arm wounds. But I have no idea what it might have been," said Remy.

"Thanks. I'll tell Sheriff Callahan." Amanda was so anxious to get this news to Callahan that she was about to hang up without confronting Remy, when he stopped her.

"Wait. There's another thing that's been troubling me," he said.

"What?" asked Amanda.

"It was something I said to you the other day at the morgue. I described Susan Gibbons in a way that was uncalled for. I wanted you to know that's not really me. We medical examiners develop a dark sense of humor because of the horror we confront almost daily. I forget myself sometimes when I talk to lay people. And I sensed I may have offended you. If I did, I want to apologize."

"You did, and your apology is accepted," said Amanda absolutely surprised.

"Thanks," said Remy, and the call ended.

"Well, I'll be darned," she said to herself and reached for her phone to call Callahan.

Chapter 20

COLLIN O'DONNELL WAS EXUBERANT as he addressed the audience fanned out over the lawn of the park beneath the lighthouse. As the county's commissioner, he had a right to be pleased. The island's annual music festival was drawing more tourists every year and becoming a boon to its economy. Last year, the nine days of the festival produced almost a fifth of the yearly income of the hotels, restaurants, and shops in the county. This year looked even better. The Nicolet Boat Company's two ferries that normally ran to and from the mainland three times a day were pressed into a fourth run for the weekdays of the festival and a fifth for the festival's two weekends. O'Donnell didn't spare the audience a single detail. He wanted everyone to hear of his brainchild's success. The audience, especially Amanda and Nick, wanted to hear the band Byways. It was Nick's favorite band.

The audience politely clapped when O'Donnell finished his speech and then roared when he introduced Byways and the bandmembers jumped onto the park's makeshift stage. Byways had survived thirty years of divorces, addictions, arrests, and bankruptcies intact to become Michigan's most popular country and western band. Its members were grizzled, unbowed, and beloved. The band launched into its signature song, and the audience cheered wildly and began to sing along.

Amanda and Nick had spread a mini banquet for two, complete with wine, on a blanket in the grass. The evening was perfect for an outdoor concert: warm with a gentle breeze and the pink of a dipping sun reflected in the bay. They raised their wine glasses to each other in a mute toast. Nick leaned over to say something to Amanda when a commotion began near the front of the audience. They heard shouting and then saw a thickening ring of people scurrying away from the center of the disruption. The band's instruments jangled into silence, and Amanda heard the lead singer barking, "Whoa, whoa, none of that, please," into the microphone.

"I'd better check this out," she said and began edging her way through the audience to the disturbance. When she broke into the area cleared by the crowd, she saw three men verbally and physically menacing two others. The two men were Bland and Abdullah. They appeared startled and alarmed and were backing away.

"I'm a deputy sheriff," said Amanda. "What's going on here?"

The three men stopped their harassment and eyed Amanda who was holding her badge in front of her. A short, wiry man led the group of three and kept bouncing on his toes in an imitation of a boxer's dance. He whipped bobbing strands of oily hair away from his eyes as he turned to face Amanda, his jaw jutting in defiance, and jabbed an arm toward Abdullah and Bland. "This here foreigner and his homo buddy don't belong here. We're just making sure they know that and don't forget it, is all. He needs to go back where he came from," he said. He made a quick feint toward Abdullah who jumped back. The two other men, who looked enough like their leader to be related, laughed and high-fived each other.

There was a heavy smell of alcohol on the leader's breath, and Amanda was sure the other two were also drunk. "It's you who needs to leave," she said.

"What? You're making us go and letting this fucking Arab stay. What's he doin' here? Ask yourself that."

"You have to go. Now," said Amanda.

"Says you and whose army," said the leader and lunged at Abdullah, shoving him hard in the chest and knocking him to the ground.

"That's enough," shouted Amanda grabbing the attacker's right arm at the wrist and twisting it behind his back while she simultaneously stuck her leg in front of his below the knee. She thrust him forward over her leg, and he nosedived into the grass. Still holding his arm, she drove her knee into his spine and pinned him to the ground. His compatriots hightailed it through the crowd and disappeared.

"If you want to press charges come to the station. This one's going to spend some time in a detention cell," said Amanda looking up at Abdullah.

*   *   *

Amanda had finished photographing, fingerprinting, and swabbing a DNA sample and was processing the paperwork for the arrest of the punk when Abdullah entered the station.

Julie got up from her desk and walked over to the counter separating the station's foyer from the work area and addressed Abdullah across it. "Can I help you?" she said.

"I am looking for Ms. Gillespie. . ." Abdullah paused and then corrected himself. "I'm sorry, I mean Deputy Gillespie."

"One moment, I'll get her," said Julie and started for the detention cells when Amanda came out of the room carrying papers in her hand. "This gentleman's here to see you," said Julie. "I can finish that for you, if you like," she added and reached out for the papers.

Amanda handed them to her. "Thanks. That would be great," she said and approached the counter.

"I'm not here to press charges and add to your burden. I'm here to express my gratitude," said Abdullah.

Amanda lifted the counter hatch and stepped through into the foyer. "No need for that. I was just doing my job," she said.

"Certainly, but the outstanding performance of your duties was a great benefit to me; and I cannot let it go unacknowledged. I fly back to Dubai in a few days. Bland is having a party on his yacht this weekend. Please come. I understand you have a friend. He must come too. I insist. To have you both there would mean a great deal to me." Abdullah made a slow bow to Amanda.

"I'm not sure," said Amanda.

"You must," said Abdullah, straightening up to his full height.

Chapter 21

"SO, WHAT WAS SHE clutching so tightly that she didn't even let go when a boat ran her over?" asked Callahan. "What could have been so important to her?"

He, Amanda, and Julie sat around Julie's desk in the work area of the station. Callahan wanted to use the rare occasion they were all together to dig deeper into the Gibbons case.

"It wasn't a flotation device. It was made of plastic," said Amanda.

"If she was holding it to her chest as the distribution of the shards would suggest and it wasn't a personal flotation device, then she wasn't swimming but treading water," said Julie.

"She may even have been trying to keep it out of the water," said Amanda.

"Or maybe dived into the water to retrieve it," said Julie.

"Or jumped overboard holding it?" speculated Callahan.

"It must have been important to her," said Amanda.

Julie nodded. "If she saw or heard the boat coming, she didn't let go of it and try to swim out of the way. She held on to it."

"So, what was it then?" said Amanda, bringing the brainstorming back to its beginning.

"Whatever it was," said Callahan, "Susan Gibbons died trying to protect it."

The station radio crackled, and then the harbormaster's voice burst through the static. "That barge is off the coast of the island and boats are starting to leave the harbor to intercept it. Thought you should know."

Julie pushed her chair back and stood. "You two better get a move on," she said. "I'll let the harbormaster know you're on the way."

*   *   *

Callahan had gotten word of the planned blockade through Max, of all people. Max had overheard an excited discussion at the Adult Day Care Center between two of the caregivers about preventing the barge from mooring on the island and had asked Julie about it. Julie had gone to Callahan, and he had called Superior Tow and Salvage to find out when the barge would be coming to the island next and to alert it to the possibility of a citizens' blockade. Amanda had then notified the harbormaster and asked him to tell them of any boats leaving the harbor around the time the barge would be approaching the island.

The barge had cleared the strait between Deer Island and Sandy Island when Callahan and Amanda spotted it. It was three miles from Pebble Bay, but already small craft zigzagged in front of it within yards of its prow wave. Giant peaks of spume leapfrogged from the stern of the tug pushing the barge as its engines churned the water to halt the barge's headway. Frantic bellows from the tug's horn thundered over the water, and smaller blasts from the surrounding boats peppered the gaps between. Callahan saw a disaster waiting to happen.

Amanda activated the Vigilant's light bar and siren and shoved the throttle forward until the engines began to scream. Within seconds, the Vigilant was hydroplaning over the water at nearly forty-five knots, heading for the swarm of boats surrounding the barge. The mere sight of a wailing projectile on a collision trajectory was enough for most of the craft to break away and head off over the water. Only three stayed harassing the tug when Amanda slowed the Vigilant and maneuvered it between the bow of the barge and the remaining boats.

Callahan turned on the loud speaker and switched it to full volume. "We are taking pictures of your boats and registration numbers. If you do not leave now, your boats will be impounded and you will be arrested."

That was all it took. The three vessels all scattered in different directions. Amanda and Callahan escorted the barge to its mooring in the bay before they headed back to the harbor.

*   *   *

As the Vigilant purred over the shallow waters along the coast, Callahan stood in the pilot house staring back at the boat's ribbon of wake.

"You okay?" asked Amanda worried that he might be facing down another bout of *mal de mer.*

"Yeah. I'm good," said Callahan. "Just thinking."

"About what?" said Amanda.

Callahan chose not to answer her question. Rather he said, "I want you to find out when that barge started coming to the island. Get the record of its route plus the dates and times of its departures and arrivals both from and to the mainland."

Chapter 22

⊚⊚

"HAVE YOU SEEN THESE flyers? They're being handed out all over town." O'Donnell scattered a handful of pamphlets across his desk toward Callahan. "And they're a drop in the bucket compared to what's happing on social media."

Callahan had seen them. They were everywhere, announcing the venues for a series of public meetings regarding threats to the island and its archipelago posed by various methods of oil drilling and the varying toxicity of the waste produced by each. A dedicated group of environmentally conscious islanders had organized the meetings at which scientists from the University of Michigan's biological and environmental station on the island would give lectures and answer questions. According to the buzz that reached Callahan, the organizers expected high attendance.

"You planning on attending?" asked Callahan.

O'Donnell chuffed derisively. "Actually, I am. I'm as concerned about the island as everyone else, but I'm getting worried."

"About what?"

"I don't want the island to become the epicenter of a protest earthquake. We don't have the resources to handle that."

"I could use another deputy," said Callahan.

O'Donnell glanced up and smiled sardonically. "The county's still paying for that boat of yours."

Callahan shrugged. "Don't you think you're blowing this out of proportion?" he said.

"Well, these demonstrations are a concern. I've heard that people from the mainland have come to the island to join the protests. They could be outside agitators. And I'm getting more and more calls from the mainland press. Did you know there was a TV crew on that barge the other day? WPBN-TV in Traverse City apparently got word of the planned blockade." Before Callahan could answer, O'Donnell said, "By the way, you did a great job there. Thanks. You and Amanda looked good on the six o'clock news."

Chapter 23

JACKSON PUMPED HIS TRAVEL mug full of coffee from the thermos at the breakfast bar of the Motel 6 before checking out. He had spent a sleepless night after waiting endless hours at the Grotto the day before in hopes that he might catch the bent man purchasing Susan's remaining painting. He hadn't, and the two extra days spent in Grand Rapids had been a wasted effort. But the failure of the stakeout and the sea of coffee he had drunk while on it were not what had kept him awake. He rarely slept anymore.

Their falling in love was not meant to happen. Personal relationships were strictly forbidden between protected witnesses and their handlers within the program. Such relationships would cloud a handler's judgement and endanger a witness. If known, they would fatally taint a witness's testimony and jeopardize the outcome of a criminal prosecution. The US Marshals Service enforced rigorous procedures to prevent such nonprofessional relationships. But he had seen it happen before with catastrophic outcomes. He was certain that he was immune. Until the service assigned him Susan's case.

He believed he and Susan might pull it off. They had planned everything so carefully; rehearsed until they were ready to spread the deceptions that would cover their disappearance together. He had planted the roots of their new identities too deep to be detected. The cyber footprints on the trail of their escape were ready to be wiped clean. No one would find them. But someone had found Susan, and now she was dead. He blamed himself. He had never experienced a passion like he had for her, never known such a power could exist. He would do anything for her. But he had failed to do what he was expertly trained to do, what his very being compelled him to do—protect her. He had overlooked something; had exposed a clue to her identity and whereabouts that someone had exploited. Now he would find that person.

He drove north toward Charlevoix and the ferry to the island. The coffee kept him alert, and the uninterrupted drone of the car's engine over the 180 miles of US Highway 131 was a white noise that uncluttered his mind and helped him think. As the road slid under him like a pulled ribbon, his thoughts focused on the bent man. What was his connection to Susan? Why had she been communicating with him? Jackson felt the skin on his face tighten. Susan's life and his had depended on her telling him everything. But she hadn't.

Chapter 24

⊚⊘

CALLAHAN, JULIE, AMANDA, AND Nick sat in a snug at the Arranmore Pub watching the two old men, one at either end of the bar. Both were perched on tall chairs and stared straight ahead over the sweating glass of Guinness in front of each of them. As they all watched, the one on the right slowly reached out with a gnarled mitt of a hand and gripped the glass. You could hear a pin drop in the pub as he wiped his lips with the back of his other hand and slowly raised the glass. When the glass reached his mouth, he took a sip; and a smattering of chortles and muffled groans filled the pub. Callahan held out his palm over the table, and Nick placed a five-dollar bill in it.

Amanda had filled Nick in on the local color. The two codgers were cousins, born a day apart. They were in their late eighties and both named Malone. They looked so alike that they were often mistaken for twins. Patrons of the pub had named them Right Malone and Left Malone after the end of the bar where they sat.

Because of a feud, the origins of which no one on the island remembered, they hadn't spoken to each other in nearly fifty years. Yet, they arrived at the pub at almost the same time every evening, taking up positions at opposite ends of the bar, rarely speaking to anyone, and ordering a single Guinness, which they nursed until closing time. Logic would dictate that the pub's owners would discourage such impecuniousness. But the opposite was true.

Their places at the bar were reverently reserved for them, and they were welcomed like astronauts returning from the moon and catered to like royalty. All this because the two old fools made thousands for the pub by winning and sometimes losing small fortunes for its patrons. It was an entrenched island pastime to come to the pub and bet on the boys: Who would be the first to take a sip, drain their glass, take a piss, or pay? The permutations were endless, thoroughly entertaining, and irresistible. Nick had not resisted, much to his chagrin.

"I'll put this to good use when I pay for the next round," said Callahan, stuffing the bill in his pocket. "Or not," he added with a smile.

"Or not what? Not use the five dollars or not pay for the next round?" asked Amanda.

"Both," said Callahan.

"That's what I was afraid of," said Amanda.

"Then want to bet again? This may wind up in someone else's hand," said Callahan, grabbing the bill from his pocket and slapping it down on the table.

All shook their heads, mostly in dismay.

"Okay. Then, to stay in everyone's good graces, I'll belly up to the bar and order a round." Callahan scooted out of the snug, and, as he stood, a man who had just entered the pub bumped him and nearly knocked him off balance.

The man braced Callahan's back with one hand to steady him and said in a barely audible voice, "Sorry, Sheriff."

"No problem," said Callahan as the man walked past him in a slow awkward stoop.

Callahan walked to the bar and stood next to Right Malone. He placed the five-dollar bill on the bar and pushed it next to Malone's glass of Guinness. "By rights I figure this is yours. *Sláinte.*" he said, wishing him good health with the Irish toast.

Right Malone covered the bill with the flat of his hand and slid it off the bar into his pocket. "Much obliged, Sheriff. *Sláinte agad-sa,*" he said in Irish, wishing Callahan good health as well.

Callahan nodded and signaled for the bartender. As he did, he noticed the image of the man who had bumped into him reflected in the mirror behind the bar. The man sat alone at a table along the wall and was staring at him. The intensity of his gaze, its focus, was different from the gawking Callahan usually experienced. He ordered the drinks and approached the man at the table.

"Do I know you?" asked Callahan.

"Pretty sure you don't," said the man.

"I saw you staring like you were wondering if you knew me," said Callahan.

"Nope. I'm just curious about people is all. Didn't mean to offend."

Callahan appraised the man a moment more and then nodded. "No offense. Enjoy your evening." He rejoined Julie, Amanda, and Nick at their table; and as he sat down, he watched the bent man leave the pub.

Chapter 25

৶৶

AMANDA GRABBED THE OFFERED hand of the crewmember and stepped into the yacht's tender. Nick was right behind her. To her surprise, the tender was nearly full of people she did not recognize. She assumed that they were guests of Bland who had flown in from the mainland. The women were all dressed elegantly, and Amanda silently congratulated herself on her choice of evening wear. After learning of the attire for the yacht party, she spent hours searching NordstromRack.com until she found something that fit her physique, taste, and pocketbook. Even at a deeply discounted designer apparel website, that wasn't easy. She had picked a grey crepe sheath with a halter neckline and asymmetrical hemline. She looked stunning even if she thought so herself. Nick certainly did, and, apparently, so did most of the men in the tender who looked at her a bit too long for the comfort of their female companions. Before she and Nick sat down, a second crewmember offered them a glass of champagne. Another couple boarded, and the tender got underway, motoring to Bland's yacht moored in the middle of the bay.

Amanda's reluctance to accept Bland's invitation and succumb to Abdullah's entreaty to attend the party was erased by Nick's enthusiasm for a special evening together and Callahan's idea that it posed an opportunity for them to determine if Bland threw the type of party where a young girl might tumble overboard.

As the tender glided farther out into the bay, it pulled away from the light of the town until the surface of the water was as black as the night sky. Surrounded by the sparkle of the stars in the sky and their perfect reflection on the water, Amanda felt as if the boat were suspended in space where there was neither an up nor down. The sensation was exhilarating but disorienting, and she had to keep her eyes on the yacht and hold tight to Nick to keep her world upright.

Minutes later, the tender sidled against the hull of the yacht, and a crewmember lowered aluminum stairs from the yacht's deck. Nick stood and helped Amanda up, and when it was their turn, they climbed the stairs. Bland waited at the top to greet each guest.

"I'm so glad you both could make it," said Bland, raising his voice to be heard over the live band playing on a deck above them. "Abdullah will be especially pleased." He pointed behind them. "You'll find drinks and hors d'oeuvres astern. Dinner will be served later. Enjoy."

Nick and Amanda acknowledged Bland's greeting and made way for the guests boarding behind them.

"I've never been on a yacht this size, short of a cruise ship," said Nick, craning his neck to scan the two decks above them.

"Me neither," said Amanda. "This is amazing."

Amanda and Nick worked their way toward the stern of the ship, past animated guests hugging the rail until they came to an open area. It served as a dance floor. A large bar stood at the far end, and tables adorned with ice sculptures lined the sides. The tables held trays of exotic morsels beautifully presented but unidentifiable except for their title and ingredients engraved on gold cards suspended above them. A crowd massed around the bar.

"Want some more champagne?" asked Nick.

"That would be great," said Amanda.

"Wait here, and I'll brave the log jam. I hope they have beer," he said as he began to step gingerly around guests holding small plates and hovering in ravenous indecision above the assorted delicacies on the tables.

Amanda felt a light touch on her elbow and turned around. Abdullah smiled at her.

"You're in the right place," he said.

In response to Amanda's confused look, he explained. "Here at this table. It contains all the delicacies from my part of the world, the United Arab Emirates."

"Oh," said Amanda, sweeping her eyes over the table.

Abdullah laughed. "Are you here alone?" he asked.

"No. I'm here with my boyfriend. He's at the bar getting us drinks," answered Amanda.

"Nick, is it?" said Abdullah.

"Yes."

"I understand that he works at the university's biological and environmental station."

"Yes," said Amanda.

"Excellent. There is someone I would like him to meet. Would you mind?" said Abdullah.

"You can ask him yourself," said Amanda as Nick, holding a drink in both hands, maneuvered passed the guests along the table and handed her a glass of champagne.

*   *   *

Abdullah did not reveal the identity of the guest he wanted Nick to meet until he had guided him and Amanda to a plush room on the upper deck where a tall grey-haired man regaled two couples. When the man saw them enter the room, he offered his audience a quick apology and broke away to greet Abdullah.

"Abe, I was wondering when we would bump into each other on this floating behemoth." He shook hands with Abdullah and then turned to Nick and Amanda. His eyes, however, were only on Amanda. "And who have you bought with you?" he asked.

"Governor, this is Amanda Gillespie and Nick Randolph. Nick is the person I told you about," said Abdullah.

Nick was floored. As soon as Abdullah had addressed the man, he had recognized him. Edward De Boer was Michigan's governor. Nick certainly hadn't expected to meet any dignitaries and was stunned to hear that Abdullah had spoken about him to De Boer. He wondered what on earth Abdullah could have said.

"I've been told you work at the environmental station on the island," De Boer said to Nick.

"Yes. The university has recently transferred me there," said Nick.

"And what is it that you do there, if I may ask?"

"Well, I am helping to develop and program its database management system."

"Sounds like a big job," said De Boer.

"Bigger than I originally thought. The university faculty at the station includes experts in a broad range of scientific disciplines, including conservation genetics, aquatic population modeling, and landscape ecology, as well as limnology and geographic information sciences and systems. There's a lot of research and a lot of data generated." Nick knew he sounded like he was puffing himself up under the guise of being informative and ceased his jabber, embarrassed.

De Boer nodded as if he were familiar with the scientific disciplines in Nick's litany and said, "Very impressive. You must know about everything that's going on there."

"Indirectly, but yes. All the data from the field and lab research comes through me." Nick kicked himself. What was it about this man that made him feel he had to impress him?

"I hear that the station's research projects involve the eastern shore of Lake Michigan, not just the island and its archipelago. Is that correct?"

"Actually, the station houses the Great Lakes Environmental and Ecological Research Institute. The target research of the institute involves the entire shoreline of Lake Michigan."

"I see," said De Boer.

Nick was finding it both surprising and refreshing that the governor appeared to be interested in the institute's research and asked, "Have you seen the most recent findings about the health of the lake?"

Abdullah shouldered in with the answer. "Those findings have been politicized," he said.

"What?" said Nick, startled by the interruption.

"The head of the institute has used its findings to fuel an attack on the creation of jobs and to stymy the economic growth of Michigan's shoreline towns and cities," said Abdullah.

The conversation had made such an abrupt turn that it took Nick a second or two to track its path. He knew that the institute's head was an environmentalist and an advocate for the ecological health of the lake but also an ethical and respected scientist. "I believe his conclusions are based on solid research and objective facts," Nick countered.

"The vehemence of his rhetoric shows otherwise. He selectively uses and skews findings to support an agenda adverse to legitimate business interests. He's not a scientist but a partisan. His research cannot be trusted," posited Abdullah.

Nick saw De Boer give a slight nod. This tacit ascent to Abdullah's rant infuriated Nick, and he felt compelled to fight against it. But before he could speak, De Boer said, "It's too festive an evening for strenuous debate. Let's just enjoy ourselves, shall we? It was a pleasure meeting you and your lovely date, Nick."

Amanda visibly chafed at De Boer's chauvinism and started to pull Nick away, but not before De Boer stepped over to Abdullah and led him by the elbow back to the couples to whom he had been chatting. Nick and Amanda were left to themselves.

*   *   *

"What just happened?" asked Nick.

He and Amanda had worked their way to the bow of the ship where the music wasn't so loud and they could talk. They leaned on the rail side by side facing the shore.

"I'm not sure," said Amanda.

"Why would Abdullah want me to meet the governor and then turn the occasion into an attack on the institute before the reason for the meeting became clear? Unless it was a set up for Abdullah to attack the institute. But that doesn't make sense. He apparently has the ear of the governor and doesn't need a pretext to express his views," Nick mused.

"You're not directly involved in the institute's research, so you don't own any of it." Amanda put air quotes around *own*. "Maybe they both wanted to see what your stance on the work of the institute is as an insider-slash-outsider, if that makes any sense. A confrontation may have been Abdullah's way of doing it in front of the governor," said Amanda. Nick looked skeptical, and Amanda added, "Maybe Abdullah believed that goading you would get a more forthright response than simply asking for your views in an out-of-the-blue meeting."

"But why?" asked Nick.

"Drilling into and near Lake Michigan is outlawed, but the political landscape is in upheaval. I don't know if you know it or not, but the governor is a climate change denier and has publicly claimed that if the climate is changing, it's not because of any human activity. He has steadfastly championed Big Oil in its efforts to change Michigan law and may see the institute as a threat to that agenda," said Amanda.

"Was the governor trying to enlist me in his cause in some way?"

Amanda watched the headlights of a lone car as it followed the curve of the shore. "I just don't know," she answered.

"Well, if he was, he wasted his time," said Nick. "Come on, let's check out this floating bacchanal."

Amanda gave him a quizzical look.

"A place of drunken revelry," he said.

Her look changed to one of skepticism.

Chapter 26

THE BENT MAN HAD registered at the hotel under the name of Tre Howard. He had paid cash for the room and shown a driver's license as an ID. Neither the name nor the driver's license belonged to him. Both had been skillfully manufactured to pass even the closest scrutiny, as had his several passports. To anyone who had a need to inquire, he was an American citizen and a resident of the state of Illinois. In fact, he was neither.

He had gone to the Arranmore Pub because he knew Callahan would be there. He had wanted his first encounter with the local sheriff to be in a public place when he was off duty and his guard would be down. He had learned in that encounter that Callahan was never off duty and that he had the instincts of a seasoned lawman. Callahan had sensed when he was being observed and that the bent man's scrutiny was more than a prurient curiosity about his face and mask. He had acted upon his instincts in approaching and appraising the bent man. The observer had become the observed. The bent man was now certain that he had to be very, very careful of Callahan.

Chapter 27

THE FIRST EVIDENCE OF the oil leak appeared as a mysterious coating on the sand and rocks of the beaches on the northeast tip of the island. Owners of the summer homes above the beaches also noticed a sheen on the water of the lake when it was calm. At first, they assumed it was some noxious discharge from one of the passing freighters. Then the news broke in the mainland media. An oil pipeline spanning the Straits of Mackinac along the floor of Lake Michigan had ruptured. It had been built in the early 1950's to bring oil from Canada to the refineries in Detroit and placed in the storm swept waters between Lake Michigan and Lake Huron. Inconspicuous, invisible, and silently operated by its owner, Peninsula Point Oil and Gas, its existence long ago erased from public memory. But not from the memory of the governor of Michigan. Empowered to shut the pipeline down by the same Michigan law that had approved it, he had refused to do so and was now defining the rupture as a minor spill that would be quickly repaired. But the specter of the

Deepwater Horizon oil spill still loomed large in the public's mind, and many of the forty million people who depended on Lake Michigan for their drinking water were beginning to get nervous.

And so was O'Donnell. He pressed the remote's power button, and the TV news channel vanished in a blink. He picked up his cell phone and dialed the sheriff's office. Julie answered the phone.

"Hi Julie, it's Collin. Is Matt there?"

"You're in luck. He just finished another call. I'll connect you," she said, and after a short wait, Callahan answered.

"Matt, I just watched the news for an update on that oil spill. It's worse than they originally suspected. The rupture's not under control, and they're reporting that the volume of the discharge is massive." O'Donnell paused for a moment and then continued. "If the bulk of that oil reaches our beaches, all hell's going to break loose."

"If anyone should worry about their shoreline, it's the people on Mackinac Island. The prevailing winds will take the spill in their direction, not ours," said Callahan.

O'Donnell detected a note of exasperation in Callahan's voice. He knew Callahan thought he was an alarmist, but he felt he was right this time about the island's reaction to the spill. "The winds shift. They do that here, you know. And besides, the oil doesn't have to flow in this direction for there to be trouble. The island is already in an uproar about the brine used on the roads and the drilling on Tom Egan's land. This will just add fuel to the flames. And not to be crass but elections are not that far off, and I want to keep this job. So do you," he said.

"Well, consider this: if things get bad enough for the governor to declare the oil spill a disaster, just think of the federal relief funds that could become available to the island," said Callahan.

"Hmmm," muttered O'Donnell.

"Would this be a good time to ask for another deputy?" said Callahan.

"A choice expletive would be appropriate, but I won't use it," said O'Donnell and hung up.

Chapter 28

CALLAHAN AND AMANDA WERE at the emergency medical center finishing their training in identifying opioid overdoses and administering the antidote naloxone when they received the call from Julie about a possible break-in at Susan Gibbon's cottage. Ben McIntyre was waiting for them on the front deck when they arrived. He hurried over to the cruiser as they got out.

"Come around back," he said and began leading them along a dirt path to the rear. "Today's the day I check the vacant rental properties," he called over his shoulder. "Soon as I came around back here, I saw this." He stopped and pointed to the back door. One of the glass panels was shattered. "I called the station right away. I didn't go in or touch anything. Thought it best I didn't."

"You did the right thing," said Callahan.

"Been here since I called the station. Doesn't appear anyone is still inside the house if it's a break-in. I didn't see any movement inside," McIntyre added.

Callahan put on his latex gloves and turned the knob. The door wasn't locked. "You wait outside while Amanda and I check the cottage," he said to McIntyre and then pushed open the door and stepped over the pieces of broken glass on the floor. "Careful of these," he said to Amanda who was right behind him.

At first glance, the interior of the cottage showed no signs of an intrusion and no evidence of ransacking or wild partying. Sometimes teens would pick a vacant rental property to drink and party in. Nothing appeared out of place, no up-turned cushions, no open cabinets or drawers, no empty bottles scattered about the floor.

"I'll look in the bedroom," said Callahan. "You check the kitchen. See if anyone's been staying here and cooked or used the plates and silverware."

The bedroom looked the same as when he and Jackson had been in the cottage. The bed was still made, and nothing appeared to have been disturbed. He left the bedroom and climbed the stairs to the loft.

"How you doin' down there?" he called to Amanda.

"No dirty dishes, open cans, or empty cereal boxes. Even the garbage can is empty. I'll go over the living room again," she called back.

Callahan surveyed the loft. None of the pictures seemed to be missing. All were where he had remembered them, including the painting of the trilliums that had so intrigued him. He picked it up and turned it over. The multi-folded note that he had reaffixed to the frame was still there. But it was not adhered with the original tape that he had reused. Instead, it had been folded only once and inserted between the canvas and the frame.

*   *   *

After McIntyre left, Callahan waited in the cruiser while Amanda finished dusting the door knob and surrounding area for finger-prints. She had already pulled out the small splinters of glass that remained in the glazing bars around the pane. She would check them for blood when they returned to the station. Callahan was now determined to find out who had been in that cottage.

Chapter 29

CALLAHAN NEEDED REMY IN a good mood. He wanted him relaxed and receptive. Experience had taught Callahan that the way to lure Remy away from his busy schedule as the island's doctor and county medical examiner was with a good lunch courtesy of the county. The bait was a table at the posh Brunswick Inn with a view across the strait to Paradise Island. The hook was a chilled bottle of Sauvignon Blanc accompanying the whitefish almandine. Remy held his head back until the drop of wine slid down to his lips, and then he wobbled the empty glass over the table as a signal to Callahan for a refill.

"I know you don't want to sleep with me, Matt, so what's this all about?" he said as Callahan poured.

"I appreciate all you do for the county and for my office," said Callahan. "I just don't express that appreciation as often as I should."

"Well, this is awfully nice of you. I didn't mean to be cynical." Remy paused. "Still, what is it you want?"

"Okay," said Callahan, throwing up his hands in a surrender of all pretense. "Your good company should be enough, but there is something I want to run by you."

"This excellent wine has bought you my attentive ear at least. Shoot," said Remy.

"It's Susan Gibbons," said Callahan.

"I thought it might be," said Remy.

"I'm investigating her death."

"Why? She died in a boating accident," said Remy.

"I've reason to believe her death may not have been an accident," said Callahan.

"How strong a reason?" asked Remy.

"A strong suspicion," answered Callahan.

"In other words, no reason at all," said Remy.

Callahan ignored his comment and got right to the point of their meeting. "If her death was declared a homicide, I'd have a legitimate reason to go deeper into this. I could subpoena evidence, get search warrants, detain and question suspects or persons of interest, even—"

Remy cut Callahan off. "You can't be serious. Are you asking me to declare her death a homicide? You know I can't do that. Not based on the autopsy I performed."

"No wait. Hear me out," pleaded Callahan. "All I'm asking is that you take another look. You found that plastic in her wounds. Maybe there's something else her body can tell us."

Before Remy could respond, the waiter arrived with their entrees. "Enjoy your meal," he said as he glided Remy's plate to the table.

But it wasn't just a plate. It was a china canvas containing a work of culinary art. The whitefish gleamed under a golden crust cradling a wreath of shaved almonds shrouded in a burgundy mist of paprika. The vegetables formed a balance of complimentary colors and textures which surrounded the fish and gave it an aura of succulence. And it smelled delicious.

"Ah," said Remy. "Presentation is everything. If this fish tastes as good as it looks, I may give your request serious consideration."

Chapter 30

M AX HELD A PEBBLE in his hand and stared down into the shallow pool of black water. He'd discovered the pool the last time he and the dog walked on the beach. Today, he came straight to it when Julie had dropped them off while she shopped. He loved to stroll the beach with the dog in the late afternoon when everyone had left for the day. He felt the beach was his special place then, and now it was even more special since he had found the pool. He was glad he could visit the beach again. For a while he couldn't. Something had happened, and Callahan had said no one could go on the beach until he said so.

Max raised his arm and held it over the pool a moment before he opened his hand and dropped the pebble. The instant it hit the water, a black cloak of resting tadpoles exploded, sending hundreds of the tailed amphibians skittering and wiggling over the bottom in every direction. Max laughed, and the dog ran over to him, circling the pool once before it ran off again. Max turned away from the pool and began following the dog down the sand.

As he walked, Max noticed a man come through the grass and onto the beach between him and the dog. The man appeared to be searching for something, looking down at the sand. Max became worried. This was his beach now. He was the one who was supposed to find things, not someone else. Max stopped, uncertain about what to do. The man looked up and saw him. Then he began walking toward him. Max didn't recognize the man and wondered if he should leave, but stood until the man reached him.

"Hi," said the man.

"Hi," said Max.

The man smiled. "You come here often?" he asked.

"Sometimes," said Max.

"Do you find things on the beach? I like to do that too," said the man.

"Yes," said Max.

"What kind of things do you find?" said the man.

"Things," said Max.

"Of course," said the man. "Me too. What do you do with them?"

"I hide them," said Max.

"Really? I like to hide things too. Where do you hide your things?" asked the man.

Before Max could answer, the dog ran to his side. It bared its teeth and began to growl.

"He doesn't seem very friendly," said the man.

"He's my friend," said Max, emphasizing *my*.

The dog started to bark and snarl, and the man stepped back. "Well, it was nice to find another explorer. Maybe we'll meet again," he said and turned and walked away.

Max watched him as he lumbered through the sand, head down, as if still searching for something.

*   *   *

When Julie and Max returned to the house, Max ran straight to his room and shut the door. He waited until he could hear his mother opening and shutting the kitchen cabinets as she put away the groceries. He then went into his closet and removed a piece of the floor molding exposing a gap between the wall and the floor. The gap was high enough to reach his hand through and big enough for hiding behind the wall all the treasures he found on the beach. There were the bleached skulls of birds, beautifully colored feathers, a gold ring, lightening glass, coins, smooth stones with perfect holes bored through the middle, and now this. He slid it from behind the wall and held it in his hands. He studied the words on it. He couldn't read them all, but knew if he could, they would tell him what it was. He didn't dare ask anyone for help. Then they would know about his treasure and might take it away. It had happened to him before, especially when he was younger. He wasn't going to let that happen again.

Chapter 31

@/@

NOT LONG AFTER NICK'S arrival at the university's biological and environmental station, he had begun campaigning for a secured system for the input, retrieval, and exchange of data and communications within the facility. To call it a campaign was being diplomatic. It was a war, a series of battles that nearly jeopardized his fledgling employment and his relationships with his bosses. The opposition to what he viewed as critical was an armory of competing economic priorities, ignorance, and arrogance—arrogance being the primary weapon. Oddly, he found that scientists were the ones most adverse to new technology foreign to their area of expertise. It took enormous effort to convince them that cyber security was a crucial element of their research. He had emerged from the conflict bloodied but victorious. Sort of. He hadn't been given all the funds he wanted, but they, plus the skills he had acquired at the NSA, proved to be enough to protect the site.

Now, he was engaged in another battle, defending their system against a persistent hacker. It proved easy compared to what he had combatted at the NSA. He was even able to trace the origin of the hacking—the IP address of a government computer in Lansing, Michigan.

*		*		*

Nick sat across the desk from Artem Zakaryan, the head of the university's biological and environmental station. Lou Simon filled the third chair in Zakaryan's small office. He was the second most senior staff member of the institution next to Zakaryan and Nick's immediate boss.

Nick still felt uncomfortable around Professor Zakaryan. Unimpressive physically with a voice raised barely above a whisper, Zakaryan had the habit of pausing a moment too long before responding to what anyone said to him. This, combined with a long-ago bout of Bell's palsy that permanently tweaked his face with a slight sardonic smile, gave everyone the sense that they were being intensely judged. Zakaryan was aware of this but did nothing to dispel anyone's discomfort. Nick had been forewarned of Zakaryan's idiosyncrasy and advised to ignore it, but he had trouble heeding the warning. Zakaryan stared at him, smiling.

"So, someone is hacking us," he finally said.

"No. Someone is trying to hack us. So far, they've been unsuccessful," said Nick. "At least presently," he added. "I'm not certain yet what may have occurred before I installed our new security system."

"Then this may have been going on for a while?" Simon had let Zakaryan ask all the questions up to this point.

"That's definitely possible," answered Nick.

"And you believe it's someone connected with the government in Lansing?" said Zakaryan in a way that sounded to Nick like an indictment of his conclusions rather than a question. He resisted the urge to be defensive.

"A government computer is being used. I'm certain of that," said Nick.

"Can you tell what they're after?" asked Simon.

Nick was waiting for this question and hoping to use the answer to reveal subtly his counterintelligence expertise. "Whoever is doing this is very skillful but not what I'd consider a professional," he said. "They've left a trail that I was able to uncover. They're interested in our upcoming *Ecological Evaluation of Lake Michigan Shoreline Tracts* and the data that was used to make our evaluations for the report."

"What?" said Simon. "That report will be publicly published next month. It contains the data we used and our research methods and results. There's nothing confidential about it." Simon shook his head, perplexed, then looked at Zakaryan for his reaction.

Zakaryan emitted a quick laugh. "I'm flattered that someone is interested in our work," he said to Simon. Then he added, "We have to assume that we have something that someone in Lansing wants to know about before that report is published. We just have to figure out what it is and who wants to know."

Zakaryan turned to Nick and stared at him. When he remained silent, Nick instinctively looked at Simon who shrugged.

"Good work," Zakaryan finally said. "Keep at it."

Chapter 32

JACKSON DECIDED TO JOG in the mornings. He needed exercise, and he wanted to keep his mind clear and his emotions on an even keel. The owner of the small beach-side hotel where he stayed recommended a trail through the woods that paralleled the shoreline for two miles and then jutted inland for another mile to Bartlett Lake. A six-mile circuit was perfect.

Jackson almost missed the trail's roadside entrance. The weathered wooden sign marking the trail was virtually invisible behind an overgrowth of pine saplings. And even if it had been fully visible, the paint had flaked off from the engraved letters announcing Dog Tail Trail, making them barely legible. He only found the entrance because another jogger emerged from the woods there as he drove by.

After a few perfunctory stretching exercises, Jackson began his jog. The trail's beginning narrowed, flanked by fluttering broadleafed trees. But in less than a hundred yards, it became a ridge between two ravines that dropped precipitously along both sides.

Crosshatchings of deadfall from moss-covered conifers filled the depressions. The conifers reached above the trail and swayed overhead. Almost imperceptibly, the ravine to his left swelled to a high, tree-clogged bluff that blocked the sun and plunged the trail into a dappled darkness. As he ran, the bluff to his left lost height, and the ravine to his right rose. He had to squint as the trail suddenly sliced through a fern-covered meadow before entering the woods again. The abrupt change of scenery startled him, and he felt as if he had been transported to another planet. He slowed his pace to better take in his surroundings.

For the first time, he realized the beauty of the island and how much Susan must have liked living on it. He thought too of how leaving it with him would have been a sacrifice for her. She had established a new life here.

A rafter of wild turkeys exited the woods and bunched up at the edge of the trail in front of Jackson. He had to stop while they cautiously stepped across the trail as if it were a pond covered in thin ice. Each bird inched forward, carefully lowering one leg to test the ground, head bobbing at the end of a long neck, before deciding it was safe to raise the other leg. Completely ignored by all, he stood just a few yards away and watched until the last turkey crossed. It took some time.

While Jackson continued running, he forced himself to face making a needed decision. As far as the United States Marshals Office was concerned, Susan Gibbons' death resulted from a boating accident. His investigation report filed with the office contained that conclusion, and the autopsy and objective facts supported it. Her file was now closed; the office would never know of their relationship nor of their plan to disappear together. But he knew in his gut that she had been murdered. He had asked for vacation time to remain on the island. On his own and off the clock, he would search for the ones responsible for Susan's death. When he found them, he would kill them. But to find them, he need Callahan's help. Callahan and his deputy knew the island and its people; knew who belonged on the island and who didn't. And Callahan also did not buy that Susan's death was an accident. Not yet. He still pursued an open file on her death. That made him an asset but also a loose cannon. Handled right, Callahan could help him. Handled wrong, Callahan could bring down his house of cards.

The trail ended in the wet grass at the shallow end of Bartlett Lake. As Jackson turned to head back, he knew what he had to do. He would tell Callahan about the purchaser of Susan's art but not the meaning of the note attached to the trillium painting. Not yet.

Chapter 33

@⁄@

THE SUN HAD PEEKED over the horizon when Callahan pulled up behind the carriage house that Amanda rented. She was waiting for him on the stairs. Callahan leaned over and pushed open the cruiser's passenger door. When Amanda climbed in, he handed her a to-go cup of coffee. "It's from the Dock Café. Advertised as the best coffee in town. Thought you might need it this early in the morning."

Amanda grabbed the coffee in both hands. "Thanks. You thought right," she said and took a sip. "And it is the best coffee in town."

They were headed to a secluded but dangerous beach on the island's north side to retrieve an abandoned canoe that had washed up between the rocks. The rip current there was treacherous with hidden boulders strewn under the water. Summer homes perched on the steep bluff above the beach. That meant that the continued presence of the canoe would be an attractive nuisance to the kids from those homes. The canoe was an accident waiting to happen, and Callahan wanted to get rid of it quickly.

Callahan had hitched a trailer to the cruiser, and as he backed out of the gravel driveway and onto the road, he carefully maneuvered the trailer so it rolled into the proper lane.

Amanda waited until Callahan was safely on the road and then said, "I've completed the file on the break-in. No prints on the door knob and no blood on the glass. Whoever broke into Susan's cottage took their time. It was not a smash and grab. The door itself was clean of prints, and the glass shards were free of any cloth fibers. My guess is that the intruder or intruders had done this sort of thing before. That would eliminate anyone from the island. Far as I know, we've no professional thieves living here. Although it could have been a tourist or someone from a vacation rental."

"Maybe, but there were things of value in the cottage that weren't taken but easily could have been. It didn't look like anything had been disturbed from the first time I was there with Jackson, except for that note attached to the frame of one of the paintings. It may be just faulty memory, but I could swear that I had multi-folded it and taped it back to the frame with the original tape. When I saw the note after the break-in, it was folded only once and wasn't taped but stuck between the canvas and frame."

"Tell me again what the note said," said Amanda.

"It was just one word, *Rahu*," said Callahan.

"Sounds like a backwards cheer," chuckled Amanda.

Callahan smiled. "Not spelled that way though," he said.

"Any idea what it means?" asked Amanda.

"None. It could be nothing, but considering Susan's history, who knows? Jackson got back from Grand Rapids yesterday. He went down there to check out the gallery where she was sending her paintings for sale. I'm meeting him at the Arranmore Pub later this morning. I want you there."

* * *

Callahan drove down a narrow fire lane until it stopped at the end of the woods along the bluff above the lake. He reached into the back seat and grabbed a coil of thick nylon rope as Amanda exited the cruiser and walked to the edge of the bluff. He caught up with her, and they both looked down a steep slope to the rocky bottom thirty feet below. The canoe had wedged itself between two boulders in shallow water about ten feet from the shore.

Callahan tied one end of the rope to a stump and pulled hard a few times to make sure it could hold their weight. Then he tossed the other end over the edge. When it hit the narrow strip of sand along the water, he said, "We can slide down this dune easy enough, but getting back up will be a pain. Let's retrieve the canoe and tie it to the rope. Then we'll scale the dune using the rope and pull the canoe up after us. What do you think?"

"Sounds like a plan," said Amanda, and she grabbed the rope and was over the side.

*   *   *

Retrieving the canoe had taken longer than they thought, and Callahan called in to Julie to tell Jackson they would be late for their meeting. Julie called back to say that Jackson was already at the Arranmore Pub waiting for them.

The pub was waking up when Callahan and Amanda arrived. The place had the early-morning look of a face reflected in a bathroom mirror—naked exposure to the probing glare of unnatural light. The waitstaff shuffled about, preparing for the breakfast crowd, sweeping the floor and folding napkins. Jackson sat at a table by the empty fireplace nursing a cup of coffee. He waved them over.

"This place sure looks different in the daytime," he said when they sat down.

"They'll dim the lighting soon and make it soothing. They turn all the lights on when they first open," said Amanda. "I used to work here as a waitress when I was in high school."

Callahan turned toward the bar and nodded, and a waitress came over to take their order. Jackson stuck with coffee; Callahan ordered two eggs over medium with bacon; and Amanda requested the farmer's skillet with extra sides of hash browns and sausage and a large orange juice. Jackson's eyes widened as the waitress took Amanda's order.

Callahan noticed his reaction and commiserated. By the standards of any culture in the world, Amanda was stunningly beautiful. Yet, she seemed untouched by her beauty; almost unaware of it. And she ate like a horse. He simply couldn't comprehend how she kept her figure.

"So, did you discover anything in Grand Rapids?" Callahan asked when the waitress left.

"I did," said Jackson. "Susan had just one art patron, a man always at the gallery on the days her paintings arrived and who purchased only the most expensive painting of the lot."

"Hmm. Did you get a name?" asked Callahan.

"Unfortunately, no. He always paid cash; never check or credit"

"A description?"

"Yes," said Jackson. "Male, as I said, white, younger than me but not by much, long dark hair, and tall but apparently burdened by a permanent stoop."

The lights dimmed, and the harsh glare morphed into a comforting glow.

"Do you believe she sent notes to him using her paintings?" queried Callahan.

"I think that's a good probability," answered Jackson.

"But that's a strange way to communicate. Why would she do it like that?" asked Amanda.

Jackson shrugged. "Maybe she wanted to guarantee her communications were secure, and this was the safest way she could think of."

"Yes, but she must have known about the encrypted messaging apps that are available for secure communications. Everybody does. She could have used any one of those," said Amanda.

"They might have used that method too, or, if not, maybe the recipient was not technologically savvy. Who knows? In any case, the written communication seems to have been a one-way street"

Jackson stopped speaking and Callahan remained silent. Both appeared to be thinking. Amanda broke the silence.

"It just occurred to me that selling her paintings was more than a way to communicate," she said.

"How so?" asked Jackson.

"It could have been a way to supply her with funds that appeared legit. Launder the money to hide the source, something like that. You said she was overpaid for her artwork."

"That's what the manager of the gallery thought," said Jackson. "I guess over time that money would add up."

"Then what was she really selling, or what was the money used for?" said Callahan. Everyone got quiet again. Then Callahan spoke.

"Miles, it's possible your man from Grand Rapids is on the island. I believe I've seen him," he said.

"What? When?" asked Jackson.

"I think he was here at the pub a couple of days ago," said Callahan. "Someone who fits that description bumped into me and watched me after that."

Jackson lightly tapped the knuckles of his right hand on the table in a staccato beat as if he were trying to come to a decision. He stopped and looked intently at Callahan. "Matt, there's something else you should know about the—"

Just then a middle-aged man in camo overalls strode into the restaurant and over to their table. He stopped and faced Callahan with his hands on his hips. "Sheriff, what the hell is my canoe doing on your trailer?" he said.

Chapter 34

⊚⊘

CAPTAIN KEVIN LYNCH PICKED up the receiver of the Island Ferry office phone and dialed the sheriff's station. When Julie answered, he said, "Julie, this is Kevin. Tell Callahan I'm not positive, but I think the man he asked me to look out for just bought a ticket to the mainland. He's sitting in the waiting room now. The ferry leaves in forty minutes." He hung up and looked out the office window into the waiting room.

The man sat on a bench along the wall with a backpack on the floor between his legs. Lynch noticed that he hadn't worn the backpack when he'd bought his ticket but had carried it into the ferry ticket office. The two twenty-something girls on either side of him sat transfixed with their eyes glued to the screens of their phones, while the man stared straight ahead with his arms resting on his thighs, hands clasped. Although he leaned slightly forward, there was nothing in front of him to see but a wall. The panoramic window overlooking the dock and the bay was to his left. Lynch couldn't decipher the expression on his face. Placid was as close as he could come to describing it, and, except for his age, he looked like a schoolboy sitting out detention. He wondered about Callahan's interest in him. But he couldn't waste time on such idle speculation. A record number of state politicians from Lansing had been arriving on the ferry and departing after touring the outer islands on Bland's yacht and partying in the evenings. It was all he and his crew could do to meet their incessant demands and professionally tolerate their boorish behavior. He had to make sure the ferry was ready for yet another load of the pricks.

*   *   *

Callahan arrived at the dock within ten minutes of Lynch's call. When he entered the ticket office, he recognized the man on the bench as the one he had confronted at the Arranmore Pub. The man also fit Jackson's description of Susan's art patron.

Callahan walked to where he sat and stood in front of him. The man did not look up but said, "Is there anything I can do for you, Sheriff?" The two girls glanced at each other and then up at Callahan.

Callahan looked around the office. Everyone in it was watching him. "If you don't mind, I'd like to talk to you outside," he said.

The man reached for his backpack and stood up but didn't reach his full height. He twisted his head to look up at Callahan, who motioned him towards the door. "After you," said Callahan.

Callahan led him to an empty bike rack in the dock loading area where there was no one around.

"What's this about, Sheriff?" said the man.

"Do you have some identification on you?" asked Callahan.

The man hesitated and then rummaged in a pouch of his backpack and pulled out a wallet. He removed a driver's license and handed it to Callahan. As he did, Callahan noticed a scar running from the bottom of his right thumb over his wrist. The scar appeared to run higher up his arm, but the sleeve of his shirt covered it. On a warm day, he had also buttoned his shirt up to the neck.

Callahan examined the license and then handed it back. "What are you doing on the island, Mr. Howard?"

"At this moment, I'm trying to leave it. But until now, I was enjoying its beauty and charm as a tourist," answered the man. "That's not a crime here I hope," he added.

"How long have you been here?"

"Five days."

"Where were you staying?'

"I rented a room at the hotel behind the church. Just over there," he said and pointed. "Would you tell me now what this is about?"

"Someone broke into one of the homes on the island. We're simply making certain inquiries."

The man turned toward the ticket office where people exited the door and headed for the ferry boarding ramp. "And of all the people you could have chosen, you picked me to question. I'm honored, Sheriff," he said.

Callahan smiled. "Thank you for your time. Glad you enjoyed your stay here," he said.

Callahan remained by the bike rack as the man proceeded to the ramp where Kevin Lynch took his boarding ticket and tore it in half. After the man stepped passed him, Lynch put the torn half of the ticket in his pocket.

*   *   *

Amanda was waiting in the cruiser when Callahan returned. She had been watching the exchange out of sight as Callahan had ordered. "What did you find out?" she asked.

"I got a name and address. And a physical marker. He has an ugly scar on the back of his right hand."

"And the way he was dressed: trousers, long-sleeved fully buttoned shirt. What's that about? It's not October," said Amanda.

"It's my guess he's hiding other injuries, or identifying tattoos, or both," answered Callahan. "With the scar and that stooped back of his, he's either been in a serious accident or led a very rough life. Did you get the photos?"

"I did," said Amanda and held up the camera resting in her lap. "Do you think we got the prints?" she added.

"We'll have to wait until Lynch gets back from the mainland with the ticket to be sure," said Callahan.

Chapter 35

CALLAHAN AND JACKSON HAD met at the station and now were heading to Susan's cottage to check Amanda's money laundering theory: Was her art patron funding something that Susan was into, that they were both into, or was he paying her for something besides art? Callahan wanted to search the cottage again with fresh eyes to see if any evidence turned up. The cottage was still technically a crime scene, and Callahan had not yet returned the key to the owner, so he considered their entry legal. They had just dropped Amanda off at the school where she was to train the teachers and staff in responding to an active shooter when Callahan received a call on his cell phone.

"You have ghosts on your island." The voice was Peter Dempsey's of the Detroit FBI office. Dempsey had headed the FBI's terrorism task force that worked closely with Callahan and Amanda in uncovering a plot to assassinate a British royal on American soil. A professional and personal friendship ensued, and Callahan came to consider him the go-to guy at the FBI.

"I don't understand," said Callahan into his cell phone.

"The prints and photos you sent. They belong to Anatoly Volkov. He's dead," said Dempsey.

"Who is Anatoly Volkov?" asked Callahan.

"Was," corrected Dempsey. "He was a very bad dude. Of Russian descent. Earned a solid reputation as a professional killer when working his way up the chain of command as a mercenary. Then a Russian crime syndicate in Thailand hired him as its enforcer. Very good at his job, too, until he died in a helicopter crash in the Phetchabun Mountains. According to witness accounts and photographs, no one could have survived; and all bodies were accounted for. That was five years ago. I've emailed you a detailed report along with photos."

"Could there be a mistake?" asked Callahan.

"What mistake do you mean? Are we mistaken about your man's identity, or are we mistaken that he's dead?" said Dempsey.

*   *   *

When the call ended, Callahan asked, "Did you hear enough of that?"

"Yes," said Jackson.

Callahan had turned on the speaker function and placed the phone on the cruiser's console when he realized who was calling.

"Did Susan tell you that this guy was still alive and that she was communicating with him?" There was no mistaking Callahan's accusatory tone.

"Matt, I swear. She said nothing about him to me or to anyone else at the service. This is a complete surprise." Jackson was shaking his head.

"So, you have no idea what their relationship might have been?" Callahan's attitude remained suspicious.

"No, and please believe me. Frankly, I'm shaken by this news," said Jackson.

Callahan turned off the pavement and onto the gravel road that fronted Susan's cottage. He remained silent the five minutes it took to reach the cottage. When he parked the cruiser, he turned to Jackson.

"Here's what I believe," he said. The US Marshals Service is responsible for placing someone on this island who has attracted people that pose a danger to its citizens. That danger is now clear and present. Someone murdered Susan, and an assassin has come looking for something she had. My job is to make sure this island is safe for the people who live and visit here. You can help me do that by telling me everything you know, or you can continue keeping me in the dark. You'd better make that decision now, and it had better be the right one."

It had become clear to Jackson that he needed Callahan as much as Callahan needed him. It was also clear that he couldn't tell Callahan what he needed to tell him without Callahan becoming suspicious of the source of his knowledge. It would be apparent that he knew far too much about Susan's human trafficking organization and her potential testimony against it for a mere handler in the Witness Security Program. He would have to give Callahan a plausible source for his knowledge and hope he would buy it. But the one thing he would never reveal to anyone, ever, was his relationship with Susan.

"I'm a member of a new division of the US Marshals Service. We investigate the death of a witness under our protection to determine if it resulted from a breach or failure of any Witness Security Program protocol. I'm investigating Susan's death to see if she, or we, did anything that might have revealed her true identity and placed her life in jeopardy. That assignment included a briefing on the organization she belonged to and her potential testimony against it." Jackson paused and waited for Callahan's reaction. The part about the division and his investigation was true. When he and Susan could no longer deny what was happening between them, he had requested a transfer to the new division, hoping to sever any connection between them. But it was too late. Their relationship had become unbreakable.

"Go on. I'm listening," said Callahan.

"We have completed that investigation. The report I filed with the service concluded that a boating accident caused her death. The known facts and autopsy supported that cause. I could come to no other conclusion at the time. But now it appears she continued to communicate with someone connected to the trafficking organization. She was never to do that. I believe that communication got her murdered, and I am here to find her killer. I need your help to do that, and you need mine. What I know can help us both."

"So, you've gone rogue?" said Callahan.

"No. I'm here on my own time but doing the business of the service. If we find credible evidence that someone murdered Susan, I'll reopen the investigation. If it turns out her death actually was an accident, then it will remain closed." Jackson checked Callahan again for his reaction and found a look of heavy skepticism even his mask couldn't hide. "Don't look at me like that. You're doing the same damn thing I am. You should have closed Susan's file, but you haven't. I've been open with you, Matt. You need to go along with this."

Callahan thought for a moment and then said, "Okay, but the second I find you've been holding back on me, you're history; and I drop a dime on you with the service."

Jackson had faced threats before and recognized the difference between the flab girdling a boast and the sharp edge of a vow. "Understood," he said.

Callahan wasn't convinced.

∗　∗　∗

Their search of Susan's cottage had been as thorough as they could make it without tearing out walls or pulling up floor boards. It was also thoroughly unproductive. They found nothing.

Chapter 36

Nick had found a place to live along Main Street. He was renting the converted attic of a spacious vacation home perched at the back of a wide lawn that gently sloped down to the edge of the bay. The landscaping consisted of nothing more than manicured grass. No tree, flower, or bush interrupted the expansive view of the water. The view alone was worth the rent to Nick. A couple with young children had inherited the house and stayed in it only a few weeks a year. The rest of the time, Nick had the place to himself. It was a perfect arrangement for him and the couple. He had great digs, and they had someone to look after the house during their absence.

He and Amanda had dinner together on the deck and then decided to take a walk to the lighthouse at the tip of the bay's crescent. The street lamps had just begun to glow, and the town had settled into a warm quiet. A quintessential time for a stroll but not for what he had to tell Amanda.

"I may be losing my job soon," he said.

Amanda dropped Nick's hand and stopped walking. "What are you talking about?"

Nick was a step ahead of her before he realized she'd stopped. He turned back to face her. "It may all be bullshit, but the governor is threatening to cut off funding to the university if it allows the station to publish our ecological evaluation of shoreline tracts."

"Why?" asked Amanda.

"He accused us of using false science and invalid data. Apparently, the governor objects to our evidence regarding the impact of climate change on the ecology of the lakeshore," said Nick.

"That's definitely bullshit," said Amanda.

"Well, the basis of the threat certainly is, but not the threat itself. Professor Zakaryan says he's been reliably informed that the governor has the votes in the legislature to cut off our funding. No funds mean no station and no job."

"Why's such a fuss being made over that report?"

"Good question. None of us at the station know for sure, but Zakaryan has a theory," said Nick. "The oil from the pipeline spill has begun to reach the shoreline, and Zakaryan wants to compile data on the spill's initial ecological impact so that we can chart any lasting effect over time. He's had his ear to the ground and believes that the powers that be don't want us to collect the data."

"Do you know what the university or Zakaryan is going to do?"

"Zakaryan refuses to be bullied. He says he's going to publish the report no matter the consequences and begin collecting data on the spill. But he may not be able to buck the university if it says no and he wants to keep his job," said Nick.

They started walking again, following the slow arc of the sidewalk along Main Street toward the lighthouse.

"If you lose your job, will you leave the island?" Amanda already knew the answer.

"I'd have to. I've got to find work in my field, and there are no other jobs on the island that would qualify."

"You could do something else," said Amanda.

Nick gave her a look of exasperation.

"Okay, okay. I just don't want you to leave."

"I don't want to leave either," said Nick.

They walked in silence until they got to the dock for the fishing boats. Amanda never stopped being amazed at the number of seagulls that stood, single-footed, along every inch of the rails and gunwales of the boats. Every gull on the island seemed to rest there in the evening wedged in tight rank like soldiers, nudging, shoving, pecking, and squawking.

"We'll work something out," said Nick.

Chapter 37

CALLAHAN SAT ON THE bed and screwed the cap back onto the tube of medication. He tossed the tube onto the bedside table next to his mask and remained sitting, hesitant to turn towards Julie. Time had not lessened the abhorrence he felt at exposing the raw ugliness of his wounds. He believed Julie when she professed that flesh melted by acid into a gargoyle's mien did not sicken her. At least, he perceived himself as having the face of a beast. The attack still flashed through his dreams: Turning at the call of his lover's name and the unbearable, unstoppable pain that burned into his soul—that still burned.

Julie patted the mattress. "C'mon. It's late. Get under the covers."

Callahan pulled the covers back and lay down.

"I'm a little concerned about Max. Have you noticed the way he's been acting lately?" Julie said.

"Nothing unusual. He seems fine to me. What have you noticed?" asked Callahan.

"He's just been sort of secretive. It's the best way I can describe it. I found a piece of paper on the floor outside his closet and put it on his desk. He had written something on it. It didn't make any sense, so I thought I could help him correct it if he wanted. When I asked him about it, he got upset. The paper's not on his desk anymore. It's gone, and he still seems upset with me."

"It's probably nothing, but I'll see if he'll talk to me about it, if you like," said Callahan. He pressed his head back into the pillow and lay staring up at the ceiling.

Julie turned out the lamp on her side of the bed. "Are you okay?" she asked.

"Sure," said Callahan.

"What are you thinking about, Matt?"

Callahan hesitated and then said, "It's just that you've never really told me about Max and you."

"You mean the how and why of Max, and how I fit into the how and why?"

Julie's immediate response surprised Callahan. It sounded defensive and set up a narrative that he did not want to follow. "I'm sorry," he said. Let's just get to sleep."

Julie took a deep breath and then sat up and turned on the bedside lamp. "No, it's me who should apologize. I want you to know more about Max and me and my marriage."

"It can wait," said Callahan.

"No, it can't." Julie took another deep breath and said, "You know I married late. It was a surprise to me. I thought I would be single forever, but then I met Sean and things took on a life of their own; and, before I knew it, there I was or there we were, betrothed. Another surprise was that Sean wanted children. It seems crazy now, but we never talked about children before we were married.

My age placed me well into the high-risk pregnancy category, but Sean was insistent and convincing. And something I had given up on as a possibility looked like it could become a reality. That's when I got pregnant.

"My doctors were adamant about amniocentesis. But there's a risk to the fetus with the test, and I wasn't sure what I would do if any abnormalities were detected. This was my only chance to have a child, and I wanted it so badly. So, I opted out of the procedure.

"I'll spare you the lurid details, but Sean blamed me for Max; and not long after Max's birth, he was gone. I've not seen or heard from him since our divorce.

"I've never regretted my decision though. Not for a second. I'm thankful for Max every day. I feel that I should be the one helping him through life, but the opposite is true. He's given me so much. He meets the challenges he faces with courage and dignity. There are times when I'm overwhelmed by his kindness and generosity. He's so forgiving and—"

"—And he saved my life," said Callahan.

Julie smiled and reached for Callahan's hand. She raised it to her lips and brushed a kiss against his skin. "Yes, and I'm eternally grateful to him for that too," she said.

*   *   *

Callahan had decided that the best way to approach Max about Julie's concern would be to start with something Max liked: grocery shopping. So, he had stopped at Foy's Market on the way to taking Max to his job at the Adult Day Care Center. As soon as they had walked through the door, Max went straight to the packaged dinner aisle. Callahan picked up a basket and followed him. Max waited for him at the far end of the aisle with three boxes of macaroni and cheese.

"You think you have enough there?" Callahan smiled and held out the basket.

Max dumped the boxes into the basket and reached for another box on the shelf. "Okay, one more," he said.

"I need to get milk for the coffee at the station," said Callahan.

"Orange juice too," said Max, and he stepped passed Callahan and headed for the coolers at the opposite end of the aisle.

"Wait," said Callahan. "I want to ask you something."

Max stopped and turned to face Callahan, jouncing slightly on his toes with impatience.

"You mother is a little worried," began Callahan.

"About what?" said Max, settling into a flat-footed stance.

"She just wanted to help you when she saw the paper that—"

Max hunched over and clinched his sides with his elbows, turning his head away from Callahan.

"Max, it's okay. I only wanted to talk with you about it," said Callahan in as soothing a voice as he could muster.

Max's body tightened, and he shook his head.

Callahan put his hand on Max's shoulder. The muscles were knotted. "Max, remember our conversation about my being the sheriff?"

"Yes," said Max.

"Then you know what my being the sheriff means, don't you?"

"You're supposed to help people if something's wrong," said Max.

"Yes. And I'm your friend too, which means I'm supposed to help you if something's wrong. Is something wrong, Max?"

"We find things," said Max.

"Who? Who finds things?" asked Callahan.

"Me and the man on the beach. We look for things and find them. He wants to know what I find, but I won't tell him. It's my treasure, not his."

"What man, Max? Do you know him?" Callahan's voice had switched from calm to urgent.

"No," said Max.

"Max, did the man want you to go with him anywhere?"

"No. The dog doesn't like him. He went away," said Max.

"Have you seen him again?" asked Callahan.

Max shook his head.

"What did you find Max?"

"I don't know what it is. If I show you, you won't take it away from me, will you? If you find things, they're yours, nobody else's. Right?"

"Yes and no, Max. If it belongs to someone and we know who, we must give it back to them. It's theirs. You know that's the right thing to do. What if you lost something and someone found it and wouldn't give it back?"

Max's body relaxed, and he looked up at Callahan.

"If you show it to me, I might know what it is. And if there's a way you can keep it, I'll make sure you can," said Callahan, trying to adopt a calming tone again.

"Okay," said Max.

"Good," said Callahan, and they started to walk down the aisle together when Callahan thought of a final question. "Max, what did the man look like?"

"Like he wanted to find things everywhere," said Max.

"What do you mean?" asked Callahan.

"Like this," said Max, bending over and looking down at the floor.

*   *   *

Max insisted that Callahan wait in the hall outside his room while he retrieved the treasure. Callahan used the wait to call Max's boss at the Adult Day Care Center and tell her that Max would be a little late due to something that was not his fault. He said that he would drop Max off soon. She told Callahan not to worry and that she understood.

When Max reappeared, he held what looked like a wadded up red rag or towel. Max stared down at it for a second and then handed it to Callahan.

Callahan almost dropped it. He had expected the weight of cloth, but the object was heavy and slipped from his grasp. He caught it with his other hand before it hit the floor. Grasping it carefully, he examined the cloth. It was tightly woven and a faint red, almost pink color. He began to gently pull it away from whatever had entangled it. As he did, he saw that the fabric was adhered to two rounded forms. It took him a moment to realize that he clutched the top of a woman's swim suit. He drew the cloth aside and saw that the shoulder strap of the suit was wrapped around a narrow metal box sandwiched between a jagged sheet of cracked and broken plastic and what looked like the remnants of an electronic circuit board.

Callahan wasn't positive, but he thought he held the hard drive from a laptop computer.

Chapter 38

JACKSON FINISHED BUTTONING HIS shirt and reached for the Styrofoam cup of coffee on the dresser. He took a sip and walked to the window of his motel room. The coffee, which he made from the two-cup electric brewer in his room, tasted rancid. But he ignored the bitterness as he looked out over the lake. The window spread wide enough to provide him a panoramic view of the water where he watched the morning ferry glide out of the bay and disappear as it turned south toward the mainland. He had been on the island long enough to establish this routine, and he looked forward to it every morning. The lake fascinated him, constantly changing from day to day, even from hour to hour. The water placid one moment and then roiling with whitecaps the next, transmuting from turquoise blue to slate gray almost imperceptibly. He had never seen a lake so massive, and it was difficult not to think of it as the ocean.

The island exerted an unfamiliar pull on him. Every place he'd lived or worked embodied overt or hidden hostility. He learned to be wary and alert for the signals of disguised or blind prejudice and the potential harm to him. But on the island, he was lowering his guard, relaxing his vigilance, experiencing a growing sense of peace. In a certain way, Jackson felt that Callahan had something to do with it. He had viewed himself as the *other*, the one who would never be fully accepted. But Callahan had trumped that view of himself. Callahan's hideous and, despite the mask, blatant mutilation appeared not to matter to the islanders. Jackson wondered if perhaps it was because they saw themselves as outsiders and different.

But he had to be careful. Susan had accepted him—totally. Or so he believed. And he had equated that acceptance with honesty. He had trusted everything she had told him; had trusted that she had told him everything. Now that trust had been shaken. She had kept her relationship with the bent man from him. What had she been hiding and why? And what did that mean for him?

*   *   *

Jackson decided to walk to the station to meet Callahan. Located on the outskirts of town, the station was about a mile and a half from the motel. The walk would do him good and help him think. As he hiked along the sand shoulder of the paved two-lane road, drivers of the oncoming cars waved to him. This island tradition made him feel welcome, and, when another car approached him, he saw the driver lift a hand. It was still raised when the car slowed and rolled toward him. He didn't see the gun or feel the bullets penetrate his chest and blow the bone and muscle out his back.

Chapter 39

❧

A MANDA PEERED THROUGH THE glass partition of the ICU and into the snarl of tubes and the glow of screens from the machines that kept Jackson alive. The mass of medical paraphernalia enveloped Jackson who was all but invisible beneath it. Forty-five minutes had passed since the time the emergency medical facility received the call from the jogger who found Jackson to the time that the island medevac plane touched down on the mainland. It took another seven minutes from the waiting ambulance to the doors of the hospital's emergency room. Amanda hoped the time was brief enough to save Jackson. She had heard the call on her radio and arrived at the scene seconds after the emergency medical technicians. She had stayed with Jackson all the way to the hospital, and she was not about to leave. Whoever had tried to kill him was not going to finish the job on her watch.

Her ring tone sounded, and she grabbed the phone from her back pocket.

"How's he doing?" asked Callahan when she answered the call.

"I'm at the ICU. He's alive, but his doctors haven't yet told me his prognosis," said Amanda.

"How are you doing?" added Callahan.

"Fine. I'm good here for as long as necessary," said Amanda.

"Great. I've contacted the Charlevoix Sheriff's Office. Sheriff Markos is sending a deputy to relieve you. I've also notified the FBI's Detroit office. An agent will be there soon. Jackson's assault is a federal crime, and the Detroit office has jurisdiction. I expect a team from the FBI to be swarming the island too. I'll have to deal with that," said Callahan. He then added, "Keep me posted on Jackson's condition and if and when he can talk," and ended the call.

*   *   *

Amanda sat down in a chair propped against the wall, leaned back, and listened to the steady hum and clack coming from the apparatus in Jackson's room. It had been a long day, and she struggled to stay awake. To keep alert, she reviewed the scene as she remembered it from the moment she had arrived there.

The paramedics were attending to Jackson when she pulled off the road behind the ambulance. He lay on the ground on his back. His fully-opened shirt exposed his chest. Amanda saw the entry wounds as one of the paramedics rolled his limp body on its side. She knew then that he had been shot. She later learned that he had been conscious when the paramedics arrived but had not been able to speak. The paramedics informed her that falling on his back in the grass and lying flat had probably saved his life. The grass and slight rise in the earth staunched the flow of blood enough from the exit wounds in his back to keep him from bleeding out before help arrived. The extent of the wounds indicated someone shot him at close range. He was lucky, they said.

The jogger who found Jackson had remained at the scene, and Amanda had learned from her that she had been jogging facing traffic, so had been on the same side of the road as Jackson. Although the road was straight and the view ahead unobstructed, she had not seen Jackson ahead of her. She heard Jackson before she saw him. Two loud moans startled her and caused her to stop and look around. It was then that she saw Jackson in the grass just off the road's shoulder. She called for help immediately. She didn't know what was wrong with him or how to help him. She didn't go near his body but waited on the road to make sure the paramedics found him right away. Before coming upon Jackson, she had jogged about two miles. In that time, only three cars passed her, all oncoming. She didn't pay attention to the drivers, although she remembered each driver had waved to her. Also, she had no recollection of the makes, models, or colors of the cars. She was sorry, but a recent argument with her boyfriend occupied her thoughts as she jogged. Although, she did remember hearing a loud crack that could have been a gunshot. At the time, she thought it was a dead branch falling from a tree in the woods alongside the road. That was a common occurrence.

Exasperation replaced fatigue and Amanda sighed. There were no homes along the stretch of road where the driver shot Jackson, so there were no other witnesses she could question. Unless Jackson could describe who shot him, they were at a dead end.

Chapter 40

WHEN NICK CONFIRMED THAT Max had indeed discovered the hard drive of a laptop computer, Callahan's instructions were succinct if not entirely naïve: retrieve the data from it. Nick responded that the outcome of that endeavor would depend on the extent of damage to the drive and how long it had endured the elements. From the look of it, Nick doubted a successful result, but felt up to the challenge.

The hard drive now rested on a table in the corner of his office at the biological station where he prepared a clean and, he hoped, uncontaminated space for the work he needed to do. He had previously removed the remains of the system board and unscrewed the plastic from the case. Wearing a surgical mask and latex gloves, he first lifted the hard drive and gently swept a brush over the case until he was satisfied that he had removed any sand granules that remained on the surface. Next, using a small battery-powered vacuum, he suctioned the table around and under the drive before detaching the cover. He held the cover up to the light and examined it. It was gouged and dented, but the metal had not been pierced—a good sign.

Then, using a magnifying glass, he peered into the guts of the drive. They had been exposed to lake water, but, as far as he could tell, no sand or dirt had penetrated the chassis—another good sign. Lake water contained no salt. Therefore, the moisture had dried without leaving any salt deposits in the drive. From what he could see, the chassis was intact. Although the hard drive sustained a scratched platter clamp and a dented actuator, the spindle and platters weren't damaged; and, if the disks were uncontaminated, he was in luck.

Nick touched the side of the actuator arm with the tip of his finger and nudged it a few millimeters. It moved easily. He applied more pressure, and the arm slid from between the platters and over to the parking ramp. All he needed to do now was to remove the platters and place them into a compatible drive. If platters rotated at 7,200 RPM when he installed that drive into a working laptop, he should be able to read whatever was written on them.

*　　*　　*

Nick placed the laptop on Amanda's desk at the station. He sat in her chair as she kneeled beside him, her hand on the back of the chair for balance. Callahan and Julie stood behind them both, leaning over Nick's shoulders, and looking intently at the computer screen.

Nick swept the palm of his hand over the screen. "These are the files on the drive, or some of them. I wasn't able to retrieve all the data, but I got a good bit of it," he said.

"Are they encrypted? Are they in some sort of code?" asked Callahan. All he could see were what looked like row after row of groups of letters followed by numbers.

"The script consists of random letters and makes no sense at all. So, it's probably encrypted. The numbers also may be part of a code.

"Do you have any idea what we're looking at then?" said Callahan. He and Julie pulled up chairs on either side of Nick and leaned in to examine the screen.

"This is just a sample from the drive, but, essentially, it's a spread sheet. The columns aren't labeled, but the first appears to be a list comprised of random letter groups. None of the groups form known words but may identify something. Some of the groups are repeated," said Nick. "The second column is a list of five and six-digit numbers. I'm not sure what the numbers represent. Maybe they too are identifiers or amounts of something. The third consists of six-digit numbers that correspond to the numbers in the second column. If I had to guess, they represent dates. The fourth column lists groups of letters that also don't appear to form words. It is followed by a fifth column that also appears to specify dates that correspond to each identifier in column four. The sixth column is a catalog of groups of letters that may also be identifiers of some sort. The columns end there."

"So, what do we make of this? if anything," said Callahan.

"Well, when I worked at the NSA, I began as an analyst. Based on my training there and put as simply as I can, this looks suspiciously like a data flow chart. The numbers in column two flow from the identifiers in column one. Column one is long but repeats only three identifiers. Those three are the source of the flow. Column three dates the flow. The identifiers in column four are numerous. However, there are only four identifiers in column six, and they are where the data terminates. If you make a chart from this analysis, this is what you get."

Nick reached into his back pocket and removed a folded sheet of paper. He unfolded it and swiveled his chair around so that his audience could view it. To Callahan, it looked like a depiction of those Fourth of July fireworks that explode in a ball of flaming trajectories that each explode again, forming their own veined orbs of fire.

"Any idea of what the identifiers represent?" asked Callahan.

"None," said Nick. "We'd have to break the code to know."

"What about the data, the numbers?" said Amanda.

"It could be numbers of emails, or texts, or items of some sort," said Nick.

"Or money," said Julie.

"Or people," said Amanda.

Callahan stood up. "Can you take the hard drive out of that computer?" he asked.

"Sure," said Nick. "You want me to do it now?"

"Please," said Callahan. "I want to keep it in the station's safe for the time being. Susan Gibbons may have been protecting what is on this drive when she died. We need to find that out, and until we do, we're going to protect it too."

Callahan left the station saying he wanted to follow up on Mrs. Hannity's complaint about cars encroaching on her lawn when they parked in front of her house. The Back Door Pub squatted at the end of her road. Her house was the last house before the pub, separated from it by a long grove of trees. The pub had become very popular and drew a large crowd, especially on Friday and Saturday nights. When the front lawn of the Back Door filled with cars, the overflow spilled onto the road in front of Mrs. Hannity's house, and some of the pub's patrons weren't too careful about how far over the shoulder they parked. The parkers disregarded Hannity's warning signs, and the pub's owner ignored her entreaties to curb the offenders. Callahan figured he'd talk to Mrs. Hannity first and then to the pub's owner to see if he could resolve the problem amicably.

In the meantime, Callahan felt happy to be alone. Brainstorming with Amanda and Julie was good as far as it went, but sometimes the whirlwind of ideas kept spinning until he could only slow it down in solitude. He needed this alone time to process things. He still had no answer to his question about the significance of the hard drive's data to Susan Gibbons' case, if any. Where and when Max found the hard drive on the beach and the fact that it was entangled in the shreds of a woman's bathing suit, all led to a strong suspicion that Susan had died clutching a computer that depicted the flow of encrypted data: people, money, or products perhaps. So, what might have she been doing with the computer? Where did she get it? Who did it belong to? And why didn't she let it sink when she faced death in the lake? He didn't have the answers to these questions, nor any idea how to find them.

Callahan passed the sign advertising the turn-off to the Back Door two-hundred yards ahead. When he came to the big white arrow pointing down Mrs. Hannity's road, he turned left. As he approached Mrs. Hannity's house, he saw that the grass on the front edge of her lawn was flattened and rutted with tire tracks. He also saw the hand painted sign that said *KEEP YOUR FUCKING CARS OFF MY LAWN. Amicable* may have been the wrong term for a solution to this problem, he thought.

Chapter 41

☺☺

GALLAGHER WAS CELEBRATING, AT least internally. From the outside, he appeared as taciturn as a bronze statue in a courthouse square. Inside, his stomach churned with excitement as he ate a second sugar-encrusted dollop of fat that passed for a donut at the Dock Café. The stars had aligned over the *Ledger* yet again. Zakaryan, from the biological station, had told him of the governor's threat to terminate the station's funding if it published its annual ecological evaluation of Lake Michigan shoreline tracts. Zakaryan wanted this information made public, very public.

Gallagher received this intelligence at the same time he learned that there were eleven other secret test wells along the Michigan coast. His story of drilling on the island had stirred up interest on the mainland, and investigative reporters from a major news agency had discovered other secret wells. Citing Michigan law, the Department of Environmental Quality steadfastly refused to reveal any information concerning the wells. The press had so notified the public. The oil spill woke up the environmental groups, and the uncloaking of the secret wells alerted them that the lake might be further threatened. Rumblings about *Big Oil* plundering the lake had already begun.

Gallagher's reportorial instincts told him that Zakaryan's news and the drilling of secret wells were connected, and he sensed another scoop for the *Ledger*. He grabbed his recorder and digital camera from his desk drawer and lifted the false bottom. He then counted out one hundred and fifty dollars from the hidden roll of cash before he headed for the door.

*   *   *

Gallagher planned to talk his way onto the rig's worksite on Egan's property in order to find out what he could from the workers there, paying for information if it came to that. What he found when he got there surprised him. There were no workers. Instead, a high chain link fence topped by razor wire surrounded the rig. Inside the fence paced a large German shepherd. Outside, a hut with a stenciled sign that read SECURITY blocked the entrance. A man emerged and approached Gallagher.

"Is there something I can help you with?" said the man whose tone and demeanor indicated that he was not about to offer any help. Gallagher noticed that he wore a blue uniform with no insignias of any kind. Trim, fit, and muscular, he was not the type of security guard Gallagher usually saw: flabby, out-of-shape, and in an ill-fitting uniform.

"I'm with the *Nicolet Ledger*, the local newspaper," said Gallagher. "'I'm interested in who's drilling here and for what."

"Can't help you there," said the man. "I've no idea."

"Then who do you work for?" asked Gallagher. "Perhaps they could tell me."

"That's none of your business. And you'd best be running along now," said the man.

"When was this fence put up?" said Gallagher.

"I said run along." The man made a lunge toward Gallagher who instinctively jumped back, almost falling. "Now get going," he said.

The dog had stopped pacing and was standing stock-still, its teeth bared and its eyes locked on Gallagher.

"Okay, no problem. Have a nice day," said Gallagher. He began walking away. He took six steps before turning around and snapping three quick pictures as the man entered the hut.

*　　*　　*

Gallagher downloaded the three photos of the hut to his computer at the *Ledger's* office and examined them. He had taken all three pictures on full telephoto. The man blocked the doorway in the second and third pictures, but in the first, he could see the interior of the hut. Someone had propped a plastic three-ring binder on a shelf on the back wall. The cover of the binder read, *Roundtree Security, Guard Manual.*

"Bingo," said Gallagher out loud.

Chapter 42

MICHIGAN STATE'S STUDENT TOURING troupe had just completed a seven-day run of *Our Town* on stage at the island's community center. Each summer, the island community anticipated the troupe's arrival, and Julie and Callahan were lucky to get tickets for the final performance. The students' level of acting amazed them, and both agreed that they couldn't have seen finer performances by professionals. The play had taken Callahan's mind off Jackson's shooting, but now, as he and Julie walked to O'Malley's, the shooting crept back into his consciousness.

"I'm worried I missed something," said Callahan.

"You're talking about Jackson?" said Julie.

"Yes," said Callahan. "What didn't I see? What am I still not seeing? Who targeted Jackson and why? I didn't see it coming—not even a hint."

"Maybe you didn't see anything because Jackson intentionally blinded you," said Julie.

"What do you mean?" asked Callahan.

"I've been wondering about Jackson too, and I've had trouble reconciling his job description with what he's actually doing," said Julie.

"Really? You'll have to explain that thinking to me," said Callahan.

"Sure, but you'll probably laugh," said Julie.

"Try me," said Callahan.

"Well, he could be like you, Matt. You never give up when you're grappling with a problem concerning the island. You're driven by something deeper than your professional duty. I've known that about you for a while. Jackson's also not giving up investigating Susan's death, and he also seems driven by something other than professional duty. But I think his motivation is different from yours. I think it's personal and intimate."

"You mean that . . ." Callahan paused, obviously looking for the right words.

"I mean that he and Susan were in a personal relationship—a serious one. And one he didn't want you to know about," said Julie.

Callahan stopped walking. He shook his head and started to speak, but Julie spoke first trying to strengthen her point.

"Don't you see? Jackson may have prevented you from discovering things that exposed that relationship; things that also may have revealed a danger to both him and Susan," she said.

They began walking again, and it was a long minute before Callahan responded to Julie's assertion. She didn't speak either, letting him marshal his thoughts. "What makes you suspect all this?" he finally said.

"I don't know. Small things, mostly subtle. Like the way he spoke of Susan to you the times I was listening. There was a weight to what he said about her that was heavier than mere empathy for someone who had died tragically, heavier than regret in losing an important witness. His body language gave away his feelings too. He seemed grief-stricken; in pain. He hid it, but I still could see it. And then there is the fact that he stayed on the island after he submitted his report."

"Why didn't you tell me this before?" said Callahan.

"I don't know. They were all just vagrant thoughts floating around in my head. They didn't gel until the shooting, and, even then, I thought it could be just my imagination."

"Maybe it's all in your head, but it's also possible you're right, so we can't dismiss it. Let's hope the doctors bring Jackson out of the induced coma soon and he survives his wounds. We've got to question him."

When they arrived at O'Malley's, Callahan reached for the door, but before he opened it, he said, "I think I'm going to need something stronger than beer in here."

"Me too," said Julie.

*   *   *

Callahan's Jameson and Julie's gin and tonic had the desired effect. The combination of the emotionally-charged play and their unsettling conversation afterwards had wound them both tight. The drinks worked to unwind them. So did the band playing in the pub. The members were older than the usual musicians at O'Malley's, so no rough or blaring sets deafened them. Julie and Callahan could hear each other talk and enjoy the music at the same time.

Callahan leaned back into the corner of the booth and stretched his legs out alongside the table. He held his drink and swirled the liquid in the glass. "I've been thinking about Max," he said.

"Yes, and?" said Julie.

"Well, I promised him I'd give back the hard drive he found, if I could. It looks like I won't be able to, and I know that will really disappoint him. So, I was thinking, what if we gave him a cell phone instead? It might help him get over the loss of something he cherished and prevent him from losing faith in me. I wouldn't want that. And it would be a good thing for him to have."

"A cell phone? I don't know, Matt. I've considered it before but have always thought better of it," said Julie.

"But why?" asked Callahan.

"A cell phone is more than just a phone. You know that. There are just too many ways that people who shouldn't be in his life can get in if he has one. There are all kinds of predators out there. I don't know if he can protect himself from that," said Julie.

"Julie, young children are given cell phones. We can put controls in place on the phone, and we can teach Max how to use it safely. He can operate a computer," said Callahan.

"I'm always with him when he's using the computer," said Julie.

"Okay, but just consider that if he had a phone, he could reach us whenever he needed to; and we could reach him," added Callahan.

"I'll think about it," said Julie in a way that made Callahan believe that she probably wouldn't. Then she smiled and said, "I like this song. Let's get up and dance."

Chapter 43

THE SAME OBSTACLE THAT Callahan faced—no witnesses—
impeded the FBI's three-person team of agents on the island sent
to investigate Jackson's shooting. The team's plan of action mirrored
Callahan's: Wait for Jackson to be removed from the medically induced
coma and see if he could tell them anything about the shooter or
shooters. Word on Jackson's condition came to Callahan from Sheriff
Markos: Jackson was now able to talk. Callahan traveled to Jackson's
bedside on the mainland before Markos informed the FBI.

As his Uber ride drove off, Callahan stood under the roof of
the large circular drive at the entrance to Charlevoix Hospital. He
watched a continuous trail of people spin in and out of the two
revolving entrance doors. He had spun in and out of a Chicago
hospital for endless weeks as he kept a vigil at the bedside of his
lover until she died from the same acid attack that disfigured him.

He had met Salima, or Sali as she wanted to be called, when he
was the Chicago Police Department's liaison with the city's Muslim

154

community. Fiercely independent, she had broken with her family's religious and cultural strictures for women and struck out on her own. They had fallen in love. Their relationship became an unbearable affront to her Pakistani family. Her younger brother, radicalized and to preserve the family's honor, had doused them with acid as they returned to their apartment from a neighborhood restaurant. Sali had died. He blamed himself.

For Callahan, his raw web of facial scars epitomized his still raw emotional scars; and when he entered the hospital, he felt his face suddenly go cold. He realized he had broken into a sweat.

Callahan walked past the visitor's desk and rode the elevator to the third floor. Markos had told him Jackson's room number and that he had stationed a Charlevoix sheriff's deputy outside it. Callahan checked in at the nurse's desk and was directed down the hall to the fourth room on the left. He didn't need the directions. A deputy in uniform sat in a chair outside the door. He greeted the deputy and showed him his badge. When he entered the room, a doctor was just leaving.

The doctor extended a hand to Callahan, and Callahan shook it. "You must be Sheriff Callahan. We were informed you were coming today," he said and then gestured toward Jackson. "Our man is quite a fighter. He's in the clear and going to make it. But it will be a while before he's a hundred percent. So, go easy."

Callahan nodded and said, "Thanks."

When the doctor was gone, Jackson said, "Have a seat." His voice sounded weak, but Callahan notice that his eyes signaled an alert mind.

Callahan pulled the room's one chair closer to the bed and sat down. "It's good to hear that news," said Callahan.

"You bet," said Jackson.

Callahan decided he wouldn't exhaust Jackson with preliminary chit chat but would get right to the point. "You have any idea who did this to you?" he said.

Jackson closed his eyes and shook his head.

"Can you describe the shooter?"

"No," said Jackson. "It happened so fast and was unexpected, obviously. I've tried to visualize what happened, but I can't even tell you if the shooter was male or female or the color or make of the car. It's just not in there." Jackson raised his arm and tapped the side of his head. "Sorry."

"Okay, let's examine it from another angle," said Callahan.

Jackson didn't turn his head on the pillow but slid his eyes toward Callahan.

"You hid your affair with Susan. What else were you hiding that prevented me from knowing that?" pressed Callahan.

"How? I . . ." Jackson's breathing became labored. "You haven't told the service, have you? You can't, please."

"Take it easy." Callahan placed his hand on Jackson's arm. "Only Amanda, Julie, and I know about your relationship with Susan. For now, anyway," he said. "Whatever you had planned for the two of you and whatever your career may mean to you now are nothing compared to the threat on your life and the danger to others. The shooter is still out there. Whoever killed Susan may still try to kill you. So, don't screw around with me this time, Miles. What did you and she know that is worth killing for?"

Chapter 44

JACKSON CLOSED HIS EYES, and his body seemed to sink deeper into the bed. His face looked drawn and his body's silhouette shrunken under the sheets.

Jackson's words began as a whisper. "We were going to run away together, disappear. We had it all planned. It would have worked, too. No one would ever have found us or discovered who we were. I made sure of that. Susan wanted a normal life, free from fear and constant vigilance. She knew that the Witness Security Program wasn't a shield to hide behind. It was just a veil that those who were after her would eventually see through and penetrate. I knew that too." The timer on his morphine auto-injector beeped. Jackson ignored it and didn't self-administer a dosage.

"You sure you're okay?" said Callahan.

"Yeah. I need to be coherent for this," said Jackson. He continued, "Susan knew the human traffic routes, how they were organized, and who managed them for the organization. They funneled most of the women and children through Dubai. It's a major hub for human trafficking. Susan also knew that all the money went through Dubai, that the amount of money made was staggering, unimaginable. What she didn't know was where the money went from there. That was heavily layered in secrets.

"The day before you found her dead on the beach, she contacted me in a panic. She said we had to leave right away. She wouldn't tell me why. But now I think I know. The note we found on the frame of her painting contained a codename. I was going to tell you about it. I tried once but . . . Anyway, *Rahu* is a Thai god. Sometimes malevolent, it must be given gifts to prevent harm. It was the codename the organization used for the head of the group that managed the organization's money laundering operations. The organization hid the members' identities well—usually through the assassination of those who talked too much or showed any signs of disloyalty. Also, the membership in the group may have been fluid to a degree. Like I said, the organization amassed astronomical amounts of money, and the temptation to skim may have been too great for some. The organization had a high internal body count. Anyway, the FBI never discovered the group's leader or hierarchy." Jackson paused and motioned with his head toward the cabinet next to his bed. "Can you hand me that cup of water?" he said.

Callahan poured water from a plastic pitcher into the cup. He waited for Jackson to raise the head of the bed before he handed him the water. When Jackson had taken a few sips, Callahan said, "And Susan was going to send Volkov a note with the codename. Why was she trying to communicate with a former mercenary and hitman for a crime syndicate, Miles?"

"I don't know. Honestly. But the painting never got sent, and Volkov never saw the message," said Jackson.

Callahan rose from the chair and walked to the foot of the bed and faced Jackson. He wanted Jackson to be able to look at him without turning his head or adjusting his body.

"Volkov's seen the note," he said. "I think he's the one who broke into Susan's cottage. Someone had tampered with the note when I checked it again."

"Shit," said Jackson.

"What was she trying to tell him?" said Callahan.

Jackson remained silent, obviously thinking, before he said, "Matt, I think she somehow discovered who *Rahu* was. I believe that's what got her killed. She didn't tell me his or her identity, but whoever killed Susan may want me dead because they thought she did. They somehow knew she was contacting me. Don't you see? They're eliminating witnesses. Because we've been working together, they may also suspect that you know too. Matt, you could be next."

Chapter 45

CALLAHAN'S VISIT HAD EXHAUSTED Jackson and made the pain worse. He decided to close his eyes and take himself to a more peaceful place, a place where the pain would find it hard to get to. He thought of Susan and the wonderful moments they shared, stolen and in secret, but nonetheless treasured. The male nurse entered his room so silently that it startled him when he touched his arm and whispered, "How you doing?"

"Pretty good, but I'm a little tired, and the pain has increased some," said Jackson.

"I can take care of that," said the nurse. "Just lay back and close your eyes again. Relax."

Jackson closed his eyes and listened as the nurse began quietly humming a tune as he moved about the room. The tune sounded familiar, but Jackson couldn't identify it. The nurse stopped moving and Jackson heard the morphine auto-injector beep. A wave of relief swept over him. Soon the pain would be gone. Already he could feel the drug starting to perform its magic. *Now what is the name of that tune?* he thought as the blackness washed over him.

Chapter 46

○○

CALLAHAN ARRIVED AT THE dock in Charlevoix in time for the 2:30
ferry to the island. He called Amanda and gave her a rundown on
what Jackson had revealed. He informed her of the warning Jackson
had given him. He also called Julie and told her to get Max and stay at
the station with him until he got back to the island. He then called
Peter Dempsey at the FBI's Detroit office. He was succinct to the point
of bluntness: Susan Gibbons' death was not an accident; Jackson's life
was still in danger; a hard drive had been found with data that may be
related to Susan's death and the attempt on Jackson's life; and there was
a suspect in Jackson's shooting still at large. In short, he needed help,
and he needed it now.

If Jackson was right, then the Gibbons investigation had become
personal in a way no other case had for Callahan. For the first time,
he felt not only a threat to himself but also to those closest to him.
Because of him, Julie, Amanda, Nick—even Max—knew information that might get them killed. His closeness to Sali had gotten

162

them viciously attacked. He had been mutilated, and she had died. He was not going to lose someone again.

*   *   *

Callahan decided to stroll around the upper deck of the ferry and enjoy the clean air and sun. At every point of the compass, he could see nothing but water. Out of sight of land, there was no cell phone service until just before reaching the island. He couldn't contact anyone, nor could anyone contact him. That should have made him nervous. He was used to being perpetually on call; constantly available in the event of emergency. Being involuntarily out of touch gave him a fatalistic view that oddly freed him from guilt and allowed him to relax. If things went south because he couldn't be reached, well, so be it. What could he do? To Callahan, it seemed a form of absolution. It allowed him to enjoy the ride.

*   *   *

The deep bellow of the ferry's horn announcing its approach to the dock jolted Callahan awake. He'd fallen asleep sitting on a bench at the rear of the upper deck. When he got his bearings, he saw Amanda waving from the dock.

She waited for him at the bottom of the gangway. "Why didn't you answer your phone? I was worried." she said when he reached her.

"Why? What's wrong?" he asked.

"Jackson's dead," she said.

"What? I was just with him. He looked weak, but the doctor said he was going to pull through."

"He died a couple of hours after you left the hospital. Sheriff Markos called me when he couldn't reach you. You must have been way out on the lake," said Amanda.

"How did it happen?" asked Callahan.

"Nobody knows yet. According to Sheriff Markos, the doctors are as puzzled as anyone," said Amanda.

Chapter 47

REMY WANTED TO SATISFY Callahan and himself that he had been as thorough as possible in the postmortem exam of Susan Gibbons. So, he reexamined the photographs he'd taken of Susan's body in search for another clue to the cause of her death. He believed the search would be in vain, but in one picture of her right arm, he detected a faint lesion he'd not seen before. It was nearly invisible and appeared in no other photos of her body. Remy suspected it might be a trick of lighting in the photo, but in a further nod to Callahan, he decided to examine her body again. In that examination, he found two other lesions on her right arm and four similar lesions on her right leg. They were all so faint that he almost missed them again.

He remembered seeing something like them before in the death of a fisherman on the lake. The fisherman had fallen overboard and been caught in his net before he drowned. When his body was retrieved, it had burns from the roping that left lesions of comparable length and grouping. If Susan had been in a net, that might explain how her severed head stayed with the rest of her body and been found on the beach next to it. It could explain other things too, thought Remy. He took his cell phone out of his shirt pocket and dialed Callahan's number.

* * *

Amanda convinced Callahan to have lunch at the Marina Market across from the docks on Main Street. It had a roofed deck with tables and chairs and, according to Amanda, the best hot dogs on the island. Callahan carried his order of a hot dog with relish and mustard and a bag of chips out to the deck and set his tray on one of the tables. Amanda followed him with her tray of a plate of fries and two hot dogs, each smothered in chili, cheese, onions, and hot peppers and sat down across from him.

Callahan expanded on his phone's screen one of the images that Remy had texted him. The lesions on Susan's arm and leg were so faint that he wouldn't have discerned them unless Remy had described their exact location and pattern for him.

"There. You see them? They're right there. Remy just discovered them," said Callahan, tracing their shape with his finger.

Amanda took the phone from him and peered at the screen. She turned her back to the sun and with the phone in her shadow, she examined the image again. "Yes, barely," she said.

"He thinks they're from a fishing net that Susan may have been caught in," said Callahan. "The pattern formed by the marks does look like netting," he added.

Amanda handed the phone back to Callahan. "It looks like netting, but I'm not so sure it's fishing netting," she said. "I've seen lots of fishing nets, and these patterns look different. They're diamond mesh, and that pattern is mostly seen on lifeline or safety netting between railings on boats, especially on family sailboats. It protects children from falling overboard and is very common. The mesh is also too open for net fishing in the lake."

"You think she somehow got these from being on a sailboat?" said Callahan.

Amanda shrugged. "Could be, but a thousand sailboats with safety netting are probably on the lake right now. So far this season, maybe a thousand more have came in and out of our harbor and sailed off to marinas all along the coast of Lake Michigan. I don't see how this helps us," said Amanda, exasperated.

Callahan looked out over the marina. At least a third of the sailboats moored at the docks had lifeline netting. He shook his head. "I've seen weaker leads pay off. We'll make one stab at following it and see where it takes us. When we're done here, I've got to get to a meeting with O'Donnell. I'm trying to wring some more money out of the county for equipment. You go talk to the harbormaster and ask if he ever saw Susan on any sailboats and, if so, which ones."

Amanda skewered Callahan with a look that said *You've got to be kidding.* "Okay, but I doubt if the harbormaster knew Susan well enough to recognize her," she said. "I doubt if he even knew her at all. I'll try to describe her for him, but she looked like a million girls that sail on boats around here."

"People have won the lottery against greater odds. Who knows, you might get lucky," said Callahan smiling and reaching for his bag of chips. "It's either that or you can face Mrs. Grant about Mrs. Delaney's incessant complaints that she won't keep her dogs on leashes in the park."

"Those dogs are pugs, and Mrs. Grant carries them around all the time in that huge purse of hers, including on her jaunts in the park. Those complaints are just part of some other feud that's going on between those two biddies," Amanda complained.

"Still gotta respond," said Callahan.

"Fine, I'll go see the harbormaster," said Amanda and pointed to her tray. "But first, I'm going to get another hot dog when I finish these."

*   *   *

"Have a seat, Matt. This is your lucky day." O'Donnell sat behind his desk, smiling and looking like a man with a secret he could hardly contain.

Callahan chose to sit on the couch facing the window rather than in one of the two chairs in front of O'Donnell's desk. He settled into it, stretched his arms along the top of the sofa's back, and crossed his legs. "Okay, out with it. What bonanza awaits me?"

"I was going to tell you that the county doesn't have the money for new equipment for your department. But that's not true anymore." O'Donnell held up an envelope. "Because in here is a $150,000 donation to the county with the stipulation that a good portion of it goes to the Sheriff's Department."

"You're kidding," said Callahan.

"Absolutely not," responded O'Donnell. "Don't you want to know who it's from?"

"I do," said Callahan.

"It comes with the grateful thanks of our visiting prince for Amanda's heroic—*heroic* is the word he used—prevention of the assault on his person at the music festival."

"Well, I'll be damned. How much do I get?" asked Callahan, bending forward.

"That is, as yet, to be determined. We must consider the needs of the entire county first," said O'Donnell.

"That's what I was afraid of," said Callahan, leaning back. Apparently, luck was liberally apportioned in Nicolet County.

Chapter 48

AMANDA HAD BEEN RIGHT about the harbormaster: He didn't know Susan Gibbons; her description fit a hundred young women in marina boats; and, in any case, he didn't keep track of the guests or temporary crew that sailed on the boats. But he did show her the bulletin board in the marina's common area with its ads for crew members and suggested she might ask the boat owners if a Susan Gibbons had responded to any of them. There was a dozen or more, but one caught her eye. The *Odyssey* had advertised for a nanny with teaching experience to care for the young children of guests during a nine-day summer cruise. The *Odyssey* was Bland's yacht. Susan would have been uniquely qualified for the job, and if the ad had been posted at the school, she might have seen it.

Amanda pulled the ad off the board and ran out of the common area. The school was just a short walk from the marina, but she couldn't get there fast enough. When she and Nick were on the *Odyssey,* she had seen a play area at the rear of an upper deck. She remembered that the railings surrounding that area had been fitted with safety netting.

* * *

Although it was summer vacation, the school's full parking lot and stream of people entering its doors signaled the building bustled with activity. Inside, Amanda passed classrooms bulging with adult education students and a gym hosting aerobic classes for seniors. She had to wait in line to meet with a frantic principal and secretary. She waited again until the secretary stole the time to print out the school's newsletters covering the dates of the *Odyssey's* marina ad. It took her only a moment to find the same ad in one of the newsletters. Amanda then pressed the secretary for the phone number of Anne Meara, the teacher she had interviewed who was Susan's friend. She called her in the hallway, and Anne verified what Amanda suspected: Susan had responded to the ad and been given the job.

Amanda's next call was to Callahan. When he answered, she skipped the preliminaries and said, "Susan was on the *Odyssey* just before she died."

Chapter 49

Gallagher researched Roundtree Security and discovered that domestic security services formed only one of the many divisions within the organization. Roundtree's services stretched around the world and included elite body guards, armed civilian contractors in Iraq and Afghanistan, and combat training for paramilitary forces in such places as Africa and Indonesia—all for big bucks. It mostly employed former military and CIA. In short, Rountree provided skilled mercenaries to the highest bidder. And it also guarded eleven other drilling sites along the coast of Lake Michigan.

Gallagher leaned back in his desk chair and smiled. His reportorial instincts had paid off once again. All organizations, especially sprawling ones, had disgruntled employees eager to slam their employer: those pissed off at a low raise, a lack of promotion, a demotion, a shitty job assignment, or firing. The list was long, and the candidates were legion. Gallagher knew he just needed to find one such employee to discover who hired Roundtree for the Eagan site. He had done just that.

Gallagher had contacted two reporters he knew from news outlets in Kalamazoo and Traverse City. He told them what he needed, and the reporter in Kalamazoo met a former Rountree drill-site guard at a bar who had been fired for drinking on the job—unjustly, or so the guy said. He'd dated a girl who worked in the head office and knew where Roundtree got its money—or some of it. After a few drinks, he loosened up and told the reporter enough so that Gallagher found out who was paying Rountree to guard the wells. It was Deep Sea Gas and Petroleum.

But that wasn't the big news. Gallagher scanned the list on his computer screen again until his eyes stopped at Infinity Cyber. Infinity Cyber held major stock in Deep Sea. And its owner was Anthony Bland. He had contacted Infinity Cyber about its connection with Deep Sea but had gotten nowhere with his inquires, nor had Bland responded to efforts to contact him about the story. Gallagher had done his part. He'd given them both a chance to refute or clarify his findings. Now, he slid to the edge of his chair and began typing on his computer's keyboard. He wanted to get the story out as quickly as possible.

Chapter 50

"I DON'T WANT TO be an alarmist, but I think it best if we're hyperalert and take certain precautions." Callahan had gathered Nick, Amanda, and Julie in his office. He didn't want to frighten them but was troubled by Jackson's disclosures. "Jackson believed that someone murdered Susan because of something she knew, and that her murderer tried to kill him because they thought he knew what she knew. Before he died, he warned me that we might be in danger, that the killer or killers were eliminating those with knowledge of that information. Because of our association with Jackson and because of our investigation into Susan's death, we may be on a hit list."

Callahan paused and checked each of them for their reaction. Julie and Nick looked concerned. Amanda just seemed curious. "There's no evidence of a connection between Susan's death and Jackson's. Jackson was speculating. Nonetheless, I want us all to be careful. Try not to go anywhere alone; keep your doors and windows locked; make sure you have your cell phones with you at all times; and contact me if you suspect you may be threatened."

Callahan turned his attention to Nick. "Collect the old hard drive parts, and all the data you retrieved and stored from its platters. I'll add it all to the drive with the platters that's in the safe." Callahan pointed to the massive steel safe on the floor in the corner of his office. Nick nodded. "Good," said Callahan. "Now Amanda and I are going to pay a visit to Bland and Abdullah."

*   *   *

Amanda swiped the screen of her cell phone for the third time and then said, "Here it is. I've got to read you this article in the electronic edition of the *Ledger*. It's about those secret drilling rigs and Bland's connection to them, or possible connection to them. The *Ledger* has uncovered the identity of the company that's doing the drilling, and it appears that Bland is a major stockholder in that company. You want to hear the article?"

"I'm listening," said Callahan.

Callahan drove as Amanda read, and when she finished reading, they had reached the turnoff onto the road that led to Bland's bunker. Callahan slowed the cruiser and then stopped, letting the engine idle. "That article gives the islanders a target for their fears about drilling in the lake, and he's right on their doorstep. Bland's going to have hell to pay here for that investment," said Callahan.

'I think his hell has already begun," said Amanda. She pointed down the road to a line of cars and trucks and a crowd gathered along Bland's property.

"Great," said Callahan.

As they approached the crowd, they saw that it was blocked at the wire surrounding the property by two uniformed guards. Several people in front were arguing with the guards.

Callahan parked the cruiser several yards behind the crowd and got out. He and Amanda shouldered their way to the front of the assembly and wedged themselves between it and the guards. Callahan held his arms above his head, and everyone quieted down.

"Glad you're here, Sheriff," said one of the guards. "We can't seem to make these people understand that no one's here. The place is empty."

"Do you know when they're coming back?" asked Callahan.

"No idea. We weren't told, and that's the truth," said the guard.

Callahan turned to the crowd and raised his voice. "Everyone, the place is empty. No one's there."

"So they say," said someone in the crowd.

"Yeah, and we have a right to be here anyway," said someone else.

"You do. And that's fine, but you don't have a right to harass these guards or trespass on this property. If you want to demonstrate or protest you can, but not on private property. These guys are just doing their jobs," said Callahan. "If you want to meet with Bland, you'll have to wait until he returns."

"When will that be?" someone yelled.

Callahan shrugged and started to speak, but Amanda grabbed his arm. "Julie called. We should get back to the station," she said.

Chapter 51

FOR AN FBI AGENT who had witnessed some of the more brutal inflictions of human butchery, Peter Dempsey was laid-back and had a gentle sense of humor. But no one would have guessed it by his appearance. He had closed-cropped black hair, a full beard, and blue eyes that pierced like needles. When you added to these physical traits the body of a gold-medal weight lifter, you got one hell of an intimidating guy. As Callahan and Amanda arrived, he was waiting in the foyer of the station sipping a cup of coffee Julie made for him. He stood and opened his arms in greeting. "Matt, Amanda, it's good to see you two again," he said.

Amanda gave him a big grin and a hug, and Callahan said, "Great to see you too, Pete. Thanks for getting here so fast."

"A federal marshal is shot on your island and is now dead; a protected witness in a major investigation washes up decapitated on your beach. Man, but you two stir up mayhem like hungry bears at a beehive. This level of chaos called for a personal appearance.

Reports from the field don't cut it." said Dempsey.

"Come in and we'll catch you up on everything," said Callahan. He raised the hatch separating the station's work area from the foyer and motioned Dempsey through. Amanda followed.

When they had settled in Callahan's office, Julie brought them all coffee, which included a second refill for Dempsey. Callahan and Amanda spent the next hour reviewing with Dempsey everything they knew about Susan Gibbons' history on the island, the circumstances of her death, her relationship with Jackson, their plan to disappear together, her communications with Volkov, Volkov's brief presence on the island, the break-in at Susan's cottage, the discovery of the hard drive and recovery of its data, and Jackson's shooting along with Callahan's belief that it and Susan's death were connected. Callahan admitted this mix included suspicion, coincidence, and even some paranoia.

Dempsey listened and let Callahan and Amanda speak without interruption until they finished. Although Jackson's relationship with Susan Gibbons surprised him, he did not telegraph his reaction. He didn't want either of them to filter what they told him. He kept his assumptions to himself. Later, he might share some and some he might not. When they'd finished, he got up from his chair and stood behind it, both hands on the backrest. He thought best on his feet.

"In spite of Jackson's fears, the facts surrounding Gibbons' death make it difficult to determine if she was murdered or not. The facts surrounding Jackson's death—not so much. Someone wanted him dead. We need to find out who and if his death was related to Gibbons'.

"I'll instruct the three agents working on Jackson's death to keep you informed of the progress of their investigation. The FBI has jurisdiction of that case. He was a federal marshal. You'll have jurisdiction over Gibbons' death unless either investigation turns up a connection between her death and Jackson's. Then we take over from there. If it turns out she may have been murdered for being a major witness in a federal criminal investigation, then that would be our bailiwick. Fair enough?"

"Fair enough," said Callahan. "And thanks, Pete."

"Finally, I'm interested in what's on that hard drive. I want to get the authority to send it to our Cryptanalysis and Racketeering Records Unit in Quantico. Our people there are pure geniuses at breaking codes. I'll set that in motion when I get back to Detroit. Until then, keep it locked up in your safe."

"Will do," said Callahan.

"Great," said Dempsey with a clap of his hands. "Now let's get some lunch. My treat. Where should we go?"

Chapter 52

DEMPSEY SCANNED THE WALL of historical photographs of the island in the terminal waiting room of Island Air. He needed to kill the twenty minutes before his flight's departure to the mainland. He hoped it would give him a brief respite from thinking about his work. At first, the collage of the island's commercial history captivated him. He followed the temporal sweep of fishing, logging, farming, homebuilding, and finally tourism pictures for a time; but eventually his mind turned back to the investigation.

The doctors were puzzled. Jackson died of a morphine overdose. The auto-injector was working properly and contained the proper amount of drug compared to the machine's data output, making it impossible for Jackson to override the injector's timed and measured doses. Yet, somehow, excess morphine had killed him.

The deputies outside Jackson's room the twenty-four hours before his death swore that only medical personnel had entered the room. The hospital's security camera appeared to confirm their assertions until further scrutiny of the recordings didn't positively identify a male nurse who entered the room. He wore loose-fitting scrubs and kept his head down and turned away from the camera while checking a clipboard. The deputy on duty outside the room glanced up from the book he was reading for only a second when the figure passed him. No nurse's notes appeared in the patient's chart for this call, and it was confirmed that the male nurses who worked at the hospital were all on duty elsewhere at this time. Jackson died a short while later amid the wailing of alarms for blood pressure, heart rate, and oxygen levels. And all this happened before Dempsey got to Charlevoix to question him.

Damn.

Dempsey chastised himself. Jackson's death upset him and not only by its timing. From everything he learned, Jackson was one of the best in the marshal's service; and his murder shocked all in federal law enforcement who knew him. That's why it had been almost as shocking to hear that Jackson had entered into a prohibited relationship with a protected witness with whom he had planned on running away. The more he discovered about people and what drove them to do the things they did, the less he understood. Their motives were never pure or clearly understood even to themselves. And because of that, he found that no one's actions were predictable. It all seemed to be a crap shoot.

Life was full of surprises, and Callahan was one of them. Dempsey had never expected to find a topflight lawman on a small, remote island in the middle of an inland sea. He had met Callahan when they worked together on a joint task force investigating a terrorist plot, and now they were united again. Callahan was a true believer. For him, justice was not an abstraction but a concrete objective. Dempsey gave up that notion long ago. For him, there was no justice, only rectification—setting things right. And that meant that the difference between him and Callahan was more than philosophical. It boiled down to methods and outcome. He hoped that this difference wouldn't cause him to run afoul of Callahan in this investigation. Whoever had the smarts and wherewithal to do away with Jackson in the hospital was dangerous. And Dempsey knew what had to be done with dangerous people, or he once did.

The speaker in the small terminal announced his flight, and he and two other people sauntered through the opened glass door, onto the tarmac, and boarded the parked plane.

*   *   *

Max took the cell phone out of his pocket for the third time in the last two minutes and looked at the picture of the dog on the home screen for a few seconds before he tapped the phone icon and then Callahan's name. The phone rang, and when Callahan answered, Max said, "Hi," and hung up. Immediately, he tapped Julie's name. The phone rang again, and when she answered, he said, "Hi," and hung up. Then he laughed. He was thrilled with the phone. No other gift was so great. His mom told him to use it only when he absolutely needed to. But he couldn't help it. It was just too amazing, and it was his. The curious metal object he'd found on the beach was all but forgotten.

Chapter 53

THE DAY WAS TOO nice for bad news. The sand along the stretch of beach glowed golden under a midmorning sun as cormorants dove and surfaced beyond the sandbars. A wary colony of seagulls skittered along the water's edge, keeping a good distance ahead of Amanda and Nick as they walked.

Amanda knew something was wrong. Nick's cheerful greeting sounded forced, and he punctuated his normally animated chat with brief but awkward silences. She wanted to know what bothered him but didn't want to prod him for an answer. She'd be patient. If he wanted to tell her, he would.

They walked along for a bit longer, and then Amanda couldn't stand it anymore. "C'mon, out with it. Something's bugging you. What is it?" she asked.

Nick hesitated and then said, "Let's just enjoy the day. It can wait."

That did it. Now Amanda had to know. "Tell me now," she demanded.

He cleared his throat, started to speak, stopped, and cleared his throat again.

"Right now," insisted Amanda.

"Okay," said Nick. "I didn't know when to tell you this or the best way to do it, but—"

"Oh no." Amanda halted, turned her back on Nick, and covered her mouth with her hand. "You're breaking up with me," she mumbled.

"What?" said Nick.

Amanda mumbled louder. "You're breaking up with me."

"No. No. Please, I didn't mean to make it sound that way. That's not it at all." It's . . . It's . . . "

Amanda dropped her hand and spun toward Nick. "It's what?" she screamed so loudly that several of the gulls took to the air screeching.

Nicks words tumbled out in one breath. "I'm losing my job. The station will shut down in a couple of months. Zakaryan didn't back down from the governor's threat. He went ahead and published our ecological evaluation of the lake's shoreline, and the legislature cut off our funding. There are no jobs for me here on the island. I'm going to have to leave. There, I've said it," he said and inhaled deeply.

"Oh. I'm so sorry," said Amanda, sounding too relieved to be sorry at all. They weren't breaking up. Then it hit her, and her relief vanished like a popped soap bubble. Nick was leaving the island.

Chapter 54

H E WAS HIDING IN plain sight.

He'd been back on the island two weeks. In that time, he'd learned the routines of the woman, Julie: when she left the house and arrived at the station; how long she worked; when and where she shopped; with whom and where she and Callahan socialized; when she went to bed and when she turned out the lights. He'd observed the timing and routes of Callahan and Amanda's weekly patrols and knew their daily schedules. He'd identified the three FBI agents on the island. And he'd learned about the boy: when he was home or at his job at the Adult Daycare Center; when he was with Julie and Callahan; and when he was alone.

He'd bought a bike in Charlevoix and taken it to the island on the ferry. Once there, he'd ridden it to a motel near the dock and rented an efficiency. He rode the bike everywhere, and when he wasn't riding, he stayed in his room. When he hunched over the handlebars, the permanent bend of his back looked natural. The helmet disguised his facial features. He rarely needed to get off the bike. He could even order groceries from the market in town along the bay and pick up and pay for his order at the market's entrance. Riding, he was just one of a hundred biking tourists on the island. He'd passed unnoticed within feet of Callahan and Amanda. He had become invisible out in the open, and it was now unlikely that his presence would be detected.

*   *   *

Bland placed the thick bind of papers in the briefcase by his feet and buckled his seatbelt in preparation for landing at Dubai International Airport. Abdullah sat in the seat across from him. Both men smiled as Abdullah's private jet began its descent.

The report was conclusive. Every test well along the coast of Michigan confirmed what industry prospectors suspected for a long time: the oil and natural gas fields in the Michigan basin extended under the lake and, by all indications, were enormous. The political winds had shifted, and shortly, directional or slant drilling would be legally allowed under the lake. Bland and Abdullah made sure of that with a massive infusion of money into the election coffers and personal pockets of certain members of the Michigan legislature. And they had a staunch ally in the governor who covertly advanced the legislative agenda legalizing the drilling. They made sure he would become a very rich man.

Bland and Abdullah had already begun leasing and purchasing the mineral rights to coastal land through shell companies financed by offshore accounts. Production wells would be erected on these lands. The potential fly in the ointment though was the revelation by that island newspaper of the existence and location of the secret test wells and Infinity Cyber's connection to Deep Sea. That disclosure caused a media stir that put the venture at risk. The price of the purchase or lease of mineral rights would go up astronomically if the results of the test drilling became known. But neither man was too worried. They could mute the media outcry and divert interest in the drilling by dismantling the wells. They were no longer needed. Through their long association, both men had become experts at risk management.

Chapter 55

SEAMUS KENNEDY'S HOUSE SAT at the far back of his lot, which bordered the main road in town. One of the oldest houses on the island, multiple generations had enlarged it by a hodgepodge of additions that made it look like a toddler's Lego Mega Block dwelling. Seamus's fourth wife divorced him twenty years ago, and he lived alone. The house was a hair's breadth shy of dilapidated. Roof tiles were missing; a variety of vermin lived in the eaves; and flakes of paint littered the grass. When the neighbors complained that it needed repair and repainting, Seamus had used sheets of tin and tar paper to cover the offending sites and adorned each addition with a different fluorescent color paint. But neither the house's appearance nor its condition caused the town's uproar. That was caused by what was on his lawn.

Seamus was a sculptor. He worked in metal, mostly iron, and his pieces were large graphic nude renderings of particular people on the island. The largest and most recognizable was his neighbor's wife. All had been arranged as a sculpture garden in his front yard, plainly visible to everyone.

After numerous warnings to remove the offending objects, the county zoning commission declared Seamus's property a nuisance and filed a civil suit against him to force compliance. Callahan was at his door to serve the complaint and summons.

Seamus opened the door and uttered a muffled, "Good afternoon, Sheriff." He swallowed a bite from the sandwich he held in his left hand and wiped his right hand on his shirt before extending it, palm up, to Callahan. "Let me have it. I knew it was coming sooner or later."

Seamus was thin, wiry, and short—very short. Callahan had to reach down to place the envelope in his hand. "You could avoid all this, you know," Callahan said.

"And why would I want to do that? I've been looking forward to it," said Seamus.

Callahan cocked his head and squinted down at him.

Seamus thrust his arms to his side and jutted his chin skyward. With his tangled crop of red hair, he looked to Callahan like an ignited matchstick. "Hell, I'm on the right side of this fight: An artist standing up to an attempt to crush his right of free expression. A battle doesn't get more righteous than that. I'm ready for it," he said.

Callahan glanced behind him at the statues and then back at Seamus. "Every one of those statues is of someone you've had a disagreement with, Seamus. If that's art at all, it's grudge art designed to humiliate, shame, and taunt."

Seamus relaxed. "Can I help it if I get my inspiration through conflict? My work is just misunderstood and unappreciated here, that's all. Hell, if it were exhibited anywhere else, it would win a prize," he countered.

"You might want to think seriously about that. Removing these statues to Minnesota would be a good idea," said Callahan.

"Hmm," muttered Seamus.

"Here's something else to think about. If I see a sculpture of me or mine on that lawn, the zoning commission will be the least of your problems," said Callahan.

Seamus glared at Callahan for a moment and then said, "No worries there, Sheriff. That ain't never gonna happen." As he closed the door, he added, "Artistic expression has its limits."

∗   ∗   ∗

Callahan chose to drive back to the station along the road that paralleled the beach where Susan's body was found. As he rounded the bend that took the road away from the lake, he saw the dog. He slowed the cruiser and then stopped. Fifty yards ahead, the dog approached him on the opposite side of the road, trotting a few yards before spinning around and skittering back, hesitating, and then trotting forward again. Its head swung back and forth, sweeping behind it with each swing as if searching for something. It was then that Callahan realized Max was not with it. The dog was alone.

∗   ∗   ∗

Callahan called out the cruiser's window to the dog, who halted, looked up at Callahan, and then became more agitated. It spun several times, started to cross the road, hesitated, and then took off, tearing along the shoulder.

Callahan turned the cruiser around and sped after the dog. When he was ahead of it, he jammed on the brakes, skidded onto the shoulder, and blocked the dog's run. The dog tried to dodge the cruiser but slipped on some gravel and slid on its side before rolling to a stop at Callahan's feet. Callahan grabbed its collar and lifted it into the cruiser.

Chapter 56

THE CALL CAME AS Julie scanned the cleaning-and-laundry-supplies aisle trying to decide which detergent to buy for the new clothes washer delivered that morning. She held two containers, one in each hand, alternating between them, comparing net weight, price, chemical composition, and promotional pitches. She dropped them both in the shopping cart and untangled herself from the strap of her shoulder bag. She opened the bag and rummaged for her cell phone. She found it on the fifth ring, and when she checked the screen, she uttered a sigh of exasperation. It was Max. For a second, she considered not answering. Max had called, said *Hi*, and then hung up a half-dozen times or more a day until threats to take the phone away had reduced his prank calls to two or three a day. But she decided against ignoring him and answered.

The voice was mechanical, artificial, neither male nor female. "If you want to see the boy alive again, do exactly as I say."

She stood paralyzed, hearing the tin voice echo in her head until the connection was severed. Then she dropped the phone and crumpled into a heap on the aisle floor.

*   *   *

Julie knelt in front of the steel safe in Callahan's office and wiped her eyes with the butt of her palm, but the tears kept welling up and blurring the numbers on the dial. Her hand shook as she attempted the combination again. She couldn't waste any more time. They hadn't given her any time. Two hours, just two hours. Again, she failed. She took a deep breath and then another and tried to block from her mind the last word she heard on her phone: a stifled scream of *Mama*. In answer to her pleas to talk to her son, they allowed her to hear only her son's primal cry of fear. She would do anything now to save him.

She squinted to squeeze the water from her eyes and steadied her hand as she rotated the dial through the sequence of numbers. At the last number, she grabbed the handle on the safe's door yanked it down. There was a metallic click, and she pulled on the handle. The door swung open.

"What are you doing?" Callahan stood in the doorway to his office. The dog nosed around him, shot over to Julie, and began licking her face.

"Oh, God. You can't be here. Go away. Please, just go away." She tried to push the dog off her and to stand but fell backwards, breaking her fall with her hands.

Callahan rushed to help her up. "What's happening? Where's Max?" he asked as he lifted her up and pushed his desk chair behind her, guiding her into it.

Julie covered her face with her hands and began sobbing. "I'm not supposed to tell you. They said they would kill him if I did. I'm not supposed to tell anyone. I don't know what to do now. I don't know what to do."

*   *   *

Between wracking sobs, Julie babbled a semi-coherent explanation of what had happened. Someone had Max. They were going to kill him if she didn't deliver the hard drive and any saved or retrieved data from it. Somehow, they knew everything was in the safe at the station. That's all she had been told, except that if she tried to get help, she would never see Max alive again. They had Max's phone, and she had heard his cry to her.

They both flinched when Julie's phone vibrated and clattered on the desk as the ringtone chimed. Callahan picked it up and looked at the number. It wasn't Max's. He handed the phone to Julie. "Answer it," he said.

Julie took the phone and tried to swipe its face, but her hand shook too much to activate it. Callahan steadied her hand with his and slid his finger across the screen. "Hello," she stammered.

"Do you have it?" The words clinked together like the links of a chain.

"Yes."

"Leave your phone at the station and get in your car and drive. Don't take any other phones or communication devices with you. And be alone. We're watching you, and we'll know."

"But, where do . . . " The call ended before Julie could finish her question, and the phone's screen faded to black.

Julie stared at the screen for a moment, and then she clutched the phone to her chest. She looked up at Matt. She wasn't crying now, and she spoke with a measured calm. "I'm going to do what they say, Matt. And you're not going to stop me. I know you're going to try, but they have Max, and I'm taking no chances, not a single one. They knew about the hard drive being in the safe. If you come with me, they'll know. If you try to get to them, they'll know. I'm getting Max back. Please don't get in my way." A tenacious resolve hovered above the tremor in her voice.

Chapter 57

JULIE BACKED HER CAR from the station's driveway and onto the road. She headed west, not because she had been told to but out of habit. It led to the house. A plastic bag on the seat next to her held the hard drive and two flash drives. She drove slowly, constantly scanning the sides of the road and checking her rearview mirror, not really knowing what to look for. It was dusk, and she had to strain to see through the trees crowding the road's narrow shoulders. Several cars passed her coming each way, but none signaled her to stop or followed her. She drove on until she reached the coast road and then turned south. Each time a car approached her, her heart would jump; and she felt sick to her stomach. Just when she thought she would have to stop and run from the car, the ringtone from a phone sounded under her seat. She slammed on the brakes and bent down under the steering wheel sweeping her hand along the floor until she felt the phone. She grabbed it and answered it before she was fully upright.

"Hello," she shouted. When there was no answer, she panicked and screamed. "Are you there?"

"You're to turn around and go back to Farmer's Road. Turn right to Glenview Road and then turn south. Drive for three miles. Stop and pull the car off the road and into the woods. Make sure no one sees you. Take what you were told to and walk through the woods until you get to a clearing. Go to the middle of the clearing and wait. You got that?"

"Yes," said Julie.

"Good. Now, throw the phone into the trees."

✳   ✳   ✳

Julie stumbled through the trees, falling several times. The sun was setting, and the dark of the woods blinded her to the brambles and branches that clawed at her legs and face. When she finally broke through the trees and into the clearing, she bled from a patchwork of scratches and cuts.

The clearing was more than a clearing. It was a huge meadow, at least a hundred yards long and almost as wide. Surrounded by woods, it formed a barren oasis in the middle of nowhere. Julie walked through the knee-high grass until she reached the center and stopped. Silence enveloped her, and the expanse and high stretch of the amber sky stripped her bare of defenses. She had never felt more exposed and vulnerable. She stood alone, thought of Jackson, and waited for the shot that would kill her.

Chapter 58

CALLAHAN STOOD IN HIS office with his finger on the wall map. "Here. Right here is where I found the dog by itself." Amanda nodded. She had raced to the station after Callahan's call and frantic explanation about Max and Julie. "It must have been chasing after Max or trying to find him when I saw it. My guess is that Max and whoever took him are somewhere around here." Callahan drew a circle with his finger on the map. "It's a stab in the dark, I know," said Callahan.

Amanda stared at the map for a moment and then pointed to a spot. "Max was on the beach here with the dog while Julie shopped. Is that what she said?"

"Yes," answered Callahan.

"Where you saw the dog is almost three miles from there. If Max was taken on the beach like Julie thinks, could the dog really have followed him that far? Isn't it more likely it was lost?"

"The dog knows its way back to the house from the beach. I don't think it was lost. I think it was trying to follow Max. It's all

198

we've got," said Callahan. "But if we find Max, maybe we can find Julie too, before they get to her. We have to try. Let's go."

"Wait," said Amanda. "That area is nothing but forest—dense forest. They won't be there. And we'd never find them there if they were. But think about it. Once they get what they want, they won't stay on the island. They'll get off as fast as they can. To do that they'd have to go by water." Amanda pointed to the area Callahan had circled. "That forest ends at the water on the east side of the island, and it's the closest point to the mainland. They'll have a boat, and they'll escape from the island there." Amanda jabbed her finger on an isolated spot on the island's shore straight east from where Callahan found the dog.

She and Callahan left the station fully armed, in body armor, and with the dog.

Chapter 59

THE BLAZE OF THE setting sun burned along the tree tops as Amanda ghosted the Vigilant along the eastern shore of the island. The light faded as Callahan scanned the beach with binoculars. This was their second time cruising along the shore of the point.

"Nothing. No boat, no footprints in the sand, nothing," he whispered.

"Should we come about and try again?" whispered Amanda.

"No. Stop here and anchor. We'll wade to the beach. Now it's the dog's turn."

*   *   *

The silence of the meadow was so complete that, at first, Julie thought the hum was the rush of blood in her ears. The hum swelled, and a dot, darker than the sky, appeared above the trees and grew larger as it floated towards her, descending until it hovered a few feet above the ground in front of her. Julie stared down at the contraption with confused fascination until the drone rose to eye level. A net basket hung beneath it, and when the drone wobbled twice, she understood she had to place the plastic bag in it. When she did, the drone shot straight up, tilted slightly, and disappeared behind her with a high-pitched whine.

Chapter 60

CALLAHAN AND AMANDA SLID over the side of the Vigilant and into the water, holding their weapons above their heads. The dog jumped in after them and paddled to shore. When it reached the beach, it zigzagged up the foredune and then dashed into the woods. Callahan and Amanda chased after it, clawing their way up the dune on all fours.

When they reached the top, they plunged into the woods after the dog and found it whining at the wall of a yellow domed tent. The entrance to the tent was zipped shut, and as Callahan moved to unzip it, the dog spun around, bared its teeth, and growled.

"Don't turn around, put your weapons on the ground, and take two steps forward. Do it now or you're both dead and so is the boy." The voice had a sinister, chilling calmness, and Callahan and Amanda obeyed. "Now the two of you get on your knees and then lay flat on the ground, arms outstretched." They both lowered themselves until they were prone in the dirt a few feet apart, their bodies extended like two plunging divers.

Callahan lifted his head. "Let the boy go," he said.

"Not possible. Not now. We had a good plan. Everything would have been fine: no problems for us and no one gets hurt. But you fucked up that scenario, Sheriff."

Out of the corner of his eye, Callahan saw Amanda's fingers slowly claw into the sand and contract. Her head was angled toward him. His nod was almost imperceptible. "It can still be that way if you leave us here and go. Kill us and you'll have problems you'll never escape," he said.

"Enough bullshit," said another voice. "Do them now."

Amanda spun on her back and heaved the sand into the faces of the two men as Callahan leaped to his feet and hurled himself up at the man closest to him.

Two shots exploded simultaneously and rang through the trees until there was silence.

*   *   *

Amanda felt a hand grasp her arm as someone lifted her to her feet. Blinded by the gun blasts, she could see only a shadow behind the orange flash that hovered in front of her eyes.

Callahan pushed up on the inert body pinning him to the ground and rolled it off him. He staggered to his feet. Two men lay face down in the dirt almost in the exact spots where Callahan and Amanda had been sprawled, the backs of their heads blown away.

"Good detective work; bad negotiating, Sheriff," said the bent man.

"It's you," said Callahan and reached down to pick up his rifle and handgun.

"The guns stay on the ground, Sheriff. You and your deputy won't need them to get back to town." Volkov raised the pistol he held in his hand and pointed it at Callahan and Amanda. He knelt over the body closest to him and searched the clothing, patting it down and feeling inside the pockets. He rolled the body over and repeated the process. He stood, stepped over the body and searched the second dead man. He found nothing on either. Then he reached into his pocket and pulled out a folding knife. He flicked it open with one hand and, keeping the gun trained on them, walked over to the tent and sliced open its side. Through the slit Callahan could see Max sitting on a sleeping bag, his wrists and ankles bound with plastic ties and his mouth taped. His eyes were wide with fear and confusion. The dog jumped through the tear and began frantically pawing Max's chest until Max toppled over.

Volkov put the knife in his belt and walked behind the bodies. He picked up the plastic bag containing the hard drive and flash drives. "I'll keep this," he said.

"What are you doing on our island?" asked Callahan.

"Paying back a debt," answered the bent man.

"And what debt is that?" asked Callahan.

"Someone saved my life and gave me a new one. I came here to save hers, but I came too late. I stayed to discover who was responsible for her death. They had her lover killed, and I knew they would come for you, the woman, or the boy. It turned out it was the boy. I was waiting." Volkov kicked one of the bodies. "These two were working for them. One or both were going to tell me where I could find them—Volkov tapped the knife—but the bastards can't talk now, can they?" He reached into the bag and held up the hard drive. "They wanted this, so this is what I will use to lure the killers out from under their rock. Then I will pay back the debt."

"You're going to kill them," said Callahan. It was a statement not a question.

"Take the boy, and the three of you get back on the boat," said Volkov.

*   *   *

Callahan pulled up the anchor, and Amanda started the engines of the Vigilant. As she motored into deeper water, they heard a large outboard roar to life beyond the point.

"Are we going after him?" asked Amanda.

"No," said Callahan. He looked at Max hunched next to him, still frightened but alive, the dog huddled by his side. "We're paying back a debt."

Chapter 61

THE TRAUMA FROM THE kidnapping had been severe for Max and Julie. Julie's uncontrollable bouts of crying and Max's crippling night terrors that began after the kidnapping continued, and she and Max were in therapy with a psychologist several times a week on the mainland. The therapist prescribed medication for anxiety and depression, which seemed to have little effect. Julie rented an apartment in Charlevoix where she and Max would stay until she felt Max was ready to return to the island. Julie didn't know how long that might be.

Callahan and the dog spent a lot of time alone together at the house with the dog whining continually, missing Max. Callahan's life didn't feel whole without Julie and Max, and he wondered if things would ever be the same for the three of them. He kept his distance while they were on the mainland. He sensed Julie wanted it that way. She had not urged him to visit them. They only talked by phone in short, strained exchanges, withholding what couldn't be said. Callahan believed Julie and Max had suffered a living night-mare because of him, and he feared that when Julie came back, she would tell him to leave.

He'd begun to drink again, alone. The whiskey set off mood swings, a catalyst to the drugs circulating inside him to keep his face from rotting and peeling away.

Callahan was about to pour himself another drink when the doorbell rang. He responded instinctively, and he was at the door opening it before he realized he didn't have on his mask. Father Martin Boucher stood on the porch looking up at him with a bemused expression.

"Caught you by surprise, did I?" he said. "Is this a bad time, or can you invite me in?" Boucher stepped around Callahan and into the house without waiting for an answer.

Callahan touched the left side of his face and then pushed the door shut and headed for the bedroom. When he came back to the living room, he had on his mask.

Boucher lounged comfortably on the couch with his legs crossed, revealing the faded jeans he wore under the brown robe of his Francis-can order. His bare toes wagged from the tips of leather sandals.

"Will you share a jar with me?" said Callahan pointing to the bottle of Jameson Irish Whiskey on the coffee table.

"*Non, merci,* unless you have Cognac. It is my downfall," said Boucher. Callahan shook his head. "Ah well. It seems no one on this island has it. *C'est la vie.*"

Callahan sat down in the chair on the other side of the coffee table from Boucher and poured himself a dollop of Jameson. He took a sip and then shrugged a silent *What's up?*

Boucher pressed the tips of the fingers of both hands together as if in prayer and was silent a moment before dropping his hands in his lap and saying, "You've heard of Irish Alzheimer's?"

"No," said Callahan, "but I'll bite. What is it?"

"They forget everything but the grudges," answered Boucher.

Callahan chuckled and nodded.

"You understand," said Boucher, smiling.

"Yes, I do," said Callahan. "I grew up in an extended Irish family, most of whom aren't speaking to each other today."

"Then you comprehend the half-truth behind the humor?" pressed Boucher.

"No, but I believe you're about to tell me."

"*Mais oui.* It has been my experience as priest on this island full of the Irish that they are slow to forgive, very slow. They eventually do but only others, never themselves. And they only half forgive. That is ironic and unthinkable for a Frenchman or even a French Canadian like myself."

"Is there a point to this, Martin?" Callahan tilted his head back, slowly draining the last finger of whiskey from his glass and then reaching for the bottle of Jameson.

Boucher leaned forward and placed the palm of his hand over the top of the bottle, preventing Callahan from picking it up. Callahan glowered at Boucher but then let go of the bottle and leaned back in his chair.

"You haven't forgiven yourself, Matt," said Boucher.

Callahan's budding friendship with Martin Boucher had sprouted on unfertile ground. He was leery of priests and had long since stopped attending church. Despite his early resistance, the friendship evolved; and he now found Martin's company comfortable and consistently enjoyable. He was grateful for it. Yet he stayed guarded, careful not to let the friendship evolve to a point where either one of them felt free to intrude upon taboo ground. He had let his guard fall only once. He had confided to Boucher of his still crippling guilt over Sali's death. That had been a mistake. It was now apparent that Boucher considered that confidence a license to push into protected space. Callahan was beginning to feel very uncomfortable.

"You're talking about Sali," he said. "Please don't."

"I'm talking about Sali and Julie," said Boucher. "And I must. After Max's kidnapping, they both haunt you, yes?"

"You want to give me absolution? Is that it? I've told you, I gave up the confessional years ago. It's not for me." Callahan shook his head. "Those who've loved me most have come to harm because of me. I could have gotten Max killed. Nothing can correct that, nothing. So don't try."

Boucher leaned forward. "You don't need absolution. You're not to blame for anything. But still you blame yourself. This is the Irish in you, *non?* I am here as your friend, not your priest. So please listen to me, Matt. We can never predict the consequences of our actions, especially those motivated by the good inside us. We can only act fearlessly and hope for the best. Evil is all around us. When it comes unbidden, we are not to blame. That's why the most powerful weapon against evil is forgiveness. *Tu comprends,* you understand?"

Callahan sighed and started to speak, but Boucher didn't wait for an answer. "You're a fighter, Matt. Use that weapon to prevent this evil from doing more harm. Don't let it destroy you or Julie. She and Max need you. Julie doesn't blame you. She knows you were trying to protect them. She's just worried about Max and still suffering for him. Forgive yourself for their sake and for yours. It will take time but start now."

Boucher sunk back into the couch and smiled. "There, I am done, *fini.* I have spoken out of turn, perhaps. So now I shall share a drop of that whiskey with you to help us both overlook my indiscretion. I suppose I must get used to its taste. *Mon Dieu,* it is the most offered drink on this island. A pity."

Chapter 62

AS THE COMMUTER PLANE descended to the Charlevoix Municipal Airport, wisps of clouds periodically blurred the view of the shoreline's sharp stretch. Callahan tightened his seatbelt as the plane bounced and swayed while it left the lake behind and flew over land. The flight from the island took no more than fifteen minutes, but he preferred the three-hour ferry ride, even in rough water. Claustrophobia and acrophobia seemed the dual goals of the plane's design and flight plan. But he chose to fly this time because he wanted to reach Charlevoix and Julie and Max before he lost his resolve about seeing them. He hadn't called or texted them first; hadn't even packed an overnight bag. He'd just given Amanda the key to the house to take care of the dog and had her drive him to the airport where he'd bought a ticket. He didn't know what he was going to say or what reaction his visit would provoke. He felt slightly sick with anxiety.

The plane bounced twice and then rolled smoothly on the runway before it began to taxi to the terminal.

*   *   *

Callahan faced the door of Room 6 that Julie had rented at the Dune Crest Inn along Route 31 outside of Charlevoix. The glare of the sun through the glass doors at either end of the hall faded to shade before reaching the efficiency unit, and Callahan stood in a pale circle of light cast down from the ceiling. The hallway was empty, and he felt isolated and alone. He raised a fisted hand twice to rap on the door and lowered it twice without knocking. He'd been standing several minutes with his arms at his side when he lifted his hand a third time and knocked.

He heard a commotion inside the room, and he stepped outside the view of the door's peephole. The door opened a few inches, and Julie peered through the crack. Then she disappeared, and the door shut. Callahan was about to walk away when he heard the chain lock slide and rattle as it fell. The door opened, and there was Julie with Max behind her. Callahan tried to speak but couldn't as he watched her eyes fill with tears.

"I've missed you," she said.

"I've missed you too," stammered Callahan.

"Where's the dog?" said Max.

Chapter 63

PALATIAL SUMMER HOMES SHOULDERED each other for prime space along the hills sloping to the shore of Round Lake, the bright blue dollop of water between Lake Charlevoix and Lake Michigan. The bridge spanning the channel which connected the small lake to Lake Michigan had opened, and boat traffic glided by the deck of the restaurant where Callahan, Julie, and Max had just finished lunch. Max waved to the people on the boats as they passed. Most waved back.

Callahan watched the activity along the ferry dock just beyond the bridge as the dock crew drove cars onto the ferry and forklifts scuttled up the loading ramp with containers of construction materials, appliances, food for the island's grocery stores, and luggage. Passengers had already started to line up for boarding. "We'd better get going. The ferry leaves soon," he said and signaled the waiter for the check. As the waiter approached, Callahan's phone rang.

He took the phone from his pocket and connected with the caller. "Callahan here," he said. He smiled a quick apology to Julie.

Julie couldn't hear the speaker's words, but she recognized the look in Callahan's eyes. The news was not good.

*   *   *

Sheriff Markos waited for Callahan outside the morgue of Charlevoix Hospital.

"Amanda said you were already in Charlevoix when I called for you on the island. Good I caught you before you left. Didn't have to drag your ass right back here. Like I said on the phone, I need you to see the guy on the autopsy table in there. Pretty sure he's the one you told us to look out for, but I need some positive visual ID. He washed up on the shore this morning in front of some expensive high-rise condos. We're still getting angry calls from the owners blaming us for not removing the body before one of the occupants discovered it. I think they're afraid it will depress the value of their units." Markos shook his head and laughed. "Like we're supposed to patrol forty miles of beach twenty-four hours a day. Come on," he said and put his arm around Callahan's shoulders and led him into the morgue.

Despite his name and its spelling, Markos was not Greek but Hispanic. To avoid any confusion regarding his ethnicity, he wore a goatee and a curled mustache. Tall with chiseled features, he was a modern-day image of Don Quixote, except that he didn't tilt at windmills. He brooked no nonsense and played by the book. He was still chafing over the fact that someone had murdered Jackson on his watch. The deputy who had guarded Jackson was no longer with the department, and Markos subsequently had every one of his deputies enrolled at Quantico in the FBI's program in protective operations.

Covered by a sheet, the body lay on a steel table in the center of the room. By its contour, Callahan knew immediately the body was Volkov's. The sheet formed a crescent: the curve of its hollow falling from a crest that followed the shape of a body on its side; Volkov's back forming the convex billow of the sheet.

Markos walked over to the table and pulled back the sheet. "There's not been an autopsy yet, but I bet he drowned and not before putting up one hell of a fight. Someone definitely wanted him dead. Take a look. Is this your man?" he said.

The body was Volkov's, and from the look of it, Callahan wondered if there might be more bodies washing up on shore. Apparently the two Volkov had killed were to rendezvous with someone on the lake. They never made it after Volkov tracked them down on the island. "Did you find anything with him, a computer hard drive specifically?" asked Callahan.

"No," said Markos, dragging out the *o* in a tinge of suspicion. "You want to tell me why you're asking?"

Chapter 64

AMANDA WATCHED AS THE tender from Bland's yacht approached and then slowed to a drift that pushed it parallel to the dock. Two of the crew stood fore and aft holding lines that they whipped over bollards to secure the craft to its mooring. Bland jumped onto the dock and walked over to Amanda.

"You here to arrest me, or is this an official welcome?" he quipped.

"Neither," said Amanda.

"That's a relief on both counts. My vast wealth usually causes me to be treated as a dignitary or a criminal." Bland smiled, but when Amanda didn't, he added, "That was supposed to be a joke."

Amanda offered a faint smile, and Bland shrugged and started to walk to the Land Rover parked at the dock's entrance.

Amanda stepped to his side and kept pace with him. "I'd like to ask you a few questions about a kidnapping on the island," she said.

Bland halted and spun toward her. "What? A kidnapping? You can't be serious," he sputtered.

"I am serious," said Amanda.

"This is preposterous. I know nothing about any kidnapping."

"Then you shouldn't have any qualms about answering my questions," said Amanda.

"This is insane. What if I refuse?" said Bland.

"That's your right. But if you do refuse, then you miss the opportunity to be removed from the list of people we want to question."

"A list of suspects, you mean?"

"You're not a suspect, only a person of interest."

"Why, for God's sake?"

"I want to see the drone you use for security here," said Amanda.

Bland's angry glare disappeared as his faced shifted to an expression of concern. "My security team doesn't use a drone anymore. About a month ago I told them to get rid of it. I saw it flying around all the time and realized those clowns were using it as a toy."

"I'd like to talk with them," said Amanda.

"They're not here anymore, at least not the same guys. A new team comes every few weeks."

"What security firm do you use?" asked Amanda.

"Roundtree Security," answered Bland. "Now, tell me who was kidnapped and if they're okay."

*   *   *

Amanda decided to walk to the lighthouse where she and Nick had arranged to have lunch together. The town's main street ended there in a circular turn-around across from the grassy park that surrounded the lighthouse. The whitewashed stone of the lighthouse formed a vivid contrast to the blue expanse of the lake, and when clouds billowed on the horizon, the view was breathtaking. The lighthouse still functioned as a navigational aid after more than a hundred years as sentinel at the mouth of the bay, but now it operated more as a popular tourist attraction. Amanda hoped that she and Nick could find an empty picnic table in the park.

Things for Nick were coming to a head, and they both were worried. His job with the university's biological station was finished; there were no other jobs on the island for someone with his qualifications; he was running out of money; and in a few days his lease would be up. Neither of them wanted to be separated, but it looked as if he had to return to the mainland and maybe even to another state to find a job. Amanda was not sleeping well, her dreams bewildering and riven by anxiety caused, she was sure, by their situation.

Nick had found a table and waved to her as she rounded the path into the park. Two adolescent gulls charged and retreated across an imaginary perimeter around the table, screeching for a tossed potato chip from him. When she got near, he stood and spread his hands over a large plastic bag from the Marina Market. "Ta da, your favorite repast—an Everything Sub." He reached into the bag, took out the bulging, paper-wrapped, footlong submarine sandwich and laid it before her on the table. "Enjoy," he said as she sat down.

Amanda unwrapped the sandwich and picked it up with both hands. She started to take a bite but stopped and said, "I don't mean to be rude, but I'm really hungry. Do you mind if I eat a little before we talk?" Then, before Nick could answer, she bit into the sandwich.

"Actually no. That was my plan in getting you your favorite lunch. I want you quiet while I speak. I have something important to say—to ask you actually—and you need to listen carefully. I've been preparing for this for a while, and I want to get it right." Nick looked at her expectantly.

Important. The word, the buildup to it, Nick's look. Could he be about to. . . Amanda's heart began to race. She stopped chewing but didn't swallow, afraid she might choke. She sat there with her mouth full of masticated bread and meat, staring at him.

"I've been thinking about this for a long time. We're so good together. It's like, you know, we sort of fit, understand each other, work well together." Amanda began to feel faint. "It's like it's meant to be—the two of us—so I'll just say it." Nick paused and then blurted, "What if I applied for the job of deputy sheriff here on the island? You said the department needs another deputy. We could be with each other, work together, and I wouldn't have to leave the island."

The wad of bread slid to the back of Amanda's throat and stuck there when her esophagus clamped shut. She couldn't breathe. She dropped the sandwich, bent over, and clutched at her chest. She started to turn blue.

"Oh my God," said Nick and jumped up from the table and ran to her. He grabbed her around the waist from the back, locked his hands together, and thrust up on her abdomen in the classic Heimlich maneuver. A gooey ball of salami-laced carbohydrate shot from her mouth and arced over the table, sending the gulls scrambling for it. She began gulping for air between bouts of hacking coughs. Nick pounded on her back.

"So, what do you think?" he asked.

Chapter 65

PETE DEMPSEY FINISHED READING the email from the FBI headquarters in DC and tried to push back against the wave of anger he felt welling up. DC had approved sending the hard drive Callahan had found to Quantico for decryption by the FBI's Cryptanalysis and Racketeering Records Unit. Headquarters had even approved expediting the process for Dempsey. That was the good news. The bad news—and there always seemed to be bad news coming with the good in this case—was that there was no longer a hard drive to decrypt.

The two men involved in the island kidnapping had been identified by their fingerprints as ex-military—former Delta Force operators. The two had opted to sign on as contractors with various security companies in Iraq, Afghanistan, and Africa before apparently going into business for themselves. Who they worked for when Volkov killed them was unknown, and that pissed Dempsey off—that and the lost hard drive. That drive contained information very valuable to someone. So far, five people had died either trying to possess that information or of being suspected of knowing the drive's contents.

Dempsey felt the muscles in his shoulders tighten and realized that he clenched and unclenched his fists. He picked up his cell phone and punched in Callahan's number.

*   *   *

Callahan felt his cell phone vibrate once in his pocket before the muffled ringtone started. Nick stopped speaking and waited for Callahan to answer the phone, but Callahan ignored the call and motioned for Nick to keep talking.

"This would be a new career path for me, a sharp turn from the one I was on, but one I know I want to take. I have a skill set that you could use. Actually, it's one that you've already used a couple of times," continued Nick.

Callahan and Nick exchanged knowing smiles. Nick was being modest in the extreme. His technical expertise had been indispensable in helping Callahan and Amanda uncover a domestic terrorism plot that had shaken the island deeply and reverberated across an ocean. Callahan had shamelessly exploited Nick's knowledge then and was doing the same now in the Susan Gibbons case. Nick's worth to the department was undeniable and demonstrable. That wasn't the problem.

"I want to stay on the island. I feel at home here, and I want to contrib—"

Callahan interrupted him. "I don't doubt any of that, but we're both ignoring the elephant in the room. You know what that is don't you?"

"You mean Amanda and me, our relationship."

"Yes. I have to consider that and how it will affect both of you working here," said Callahan. "What if—"

Now Nick did the interrupting. "—Amanda and I broke up, you mean? Could we still work together?"

"Well, yes. Or what if—"

"—our relationship affected our professional judgement?" Nick said, finishing Callahan's sentence.

Callahan looked at Nick for a long second. "You've obviously thought about this," he said.

"Yes," said Nick.

"And you and Amanda have talked it over?" said Callahan.

"Yes," said Nick again.

"How does she feel about it?" asked Callahan.

"You know Amanda, how intelligent and thoughtful she is—and how devoted she is to you. She would always put the welfare of the department and the people of this island above her own. So, she is conflicted and has reservations. The same ones you have and even more. I don't want to speak for her, but I will tell you that I wouldn't be here if she didn't want me to be. I will also tell you that I'm being the selfish one, not her. This was my idea, and she was originally against it."

Nick was being very persuasive, but Callahan wanted to be certain that the decision he made was the right one for the office and the island it served. He needed time to deliberate. "I won't pretend I don't need another deputy. I do, and any sheriff's department would be very lucky to have you. But I want to think about it," said Callahan. He stood up from the desk. "I have to go see Mrs. Hannity—for the third time. Someone has splattered raw eggs on cars that park in front of her house, and I suspect she may know something about that. Can I give you a lift somewhere?" asked Callahan.

"No thanks. I biked here, but I appreciate the offer."

"Then I'll walk you outside," said Callahan.

On the steps outside the station, Nick touched Callahan's shoulder and said, "Wait, I forgot something." He reached into his pocket, and then extended an open hand to Callahan. In his palm was a flash drive. "I thought I'd given you everything I had that contained any data from that hard drive. I loaded a copy of the flow chart I showed you onto this along with other data from the hard drive that I used to create the chart. Then I forgot about it. I only discovered what I'd done when I went to download other stuff on this drive. Sorry. Do you need it?"

Callahan beheld Nick's hand as if it cradled a ten-carat diamond.

Chapter 66

⊚⁄⊚

JULIE AND MAX HAD comfortably settled back into their lives after returning from the mainland: Julie as dispatcher and administrative head of the station, Max in his job at the Adult Day Care Center, and both as a family again with Callahan. Familiarity, routine, and a recaptured closeness were drawing all of them toward their former happiness, including the dog.

Julie took a sip of tea. "That's so sweet, Matt. It really touches my heart," she said.

"What? Nick applying for a job here? That's sweet?" said Callahan perplexed.

"Well, I do think that is sweet too, but it isn't what I meant."

"What then?" asked Callahan.

Julie put the cup of tea down on her desk. She and Callahan were alone together in the station, and he had told her there was something important he wanted to discuss with her. She knew from the way he'd asked her to *sit down a moment* so that he could *run something by her*, that what he really wanted was someone who would listen while he thought out loud. There was unlikely to be any *discussion*. So, she had made tea for them both while he got his thoughts in order, and she prepared herself to be an attentive sounding board.

Callahan had ended their tête-á-tête the way he began it. Nick's working in the department was too problematic. As much as he needed another deputy, especially one like Nick, he just couldn't have two deputies who were in a relationship in the same department. Their relationship might jeopardize their jobs, and their jobs might jeopardize their relationship. He came up with a half-dozen examples for each scenario to show how and why it wouldn't work. Finished, Callahan now sat on the other side of Julie's desk waiting for her to bless him with her wholehearted agreement. He wasn't getting it.

"It's rather endearing how your love has blinded you, Matt."

"What on earth are you talking about?"

"Your love for me. It's blinded you. Open your eyes. We're in a relationship. We work together and live together. We've survived and so has the department. When there are problems, we work them out. Even big problems." Julie paused to let that sink in and gave Callahan a steady look.

Callahan tried to meet her gaze but averted his eyes after a second. "I know," he said. "I know."

"They're in love; they will too," continued Julie. "So, lighten up and hire Nick after he's completed his courses and passed the deputy's exam. You need him."

*   *   *

When Callahan and Julie had finished their tea, he had gone back to his office to complete neglected paperwork. Instead, he sat at his desk mulling over what Julie had said. He had fretted about hiring Amanda too. Her desire and her full-on pursuit to become a deputy almost convinced him, but her youth and lack of law enforcement experience posed insurmountable obstacles. Ultimately, circumstances forced his hand, and he hired her. From that moment on, he never regretted it. In short order, she became one of the finest and smartest officers he had ever worked with. Now, he couldn't imagine doing his job without her. He trusted her in every detail of the duties they performed. He'd even trusted her with his life. Perhaps he should listen to Julie and stop fretting about Nick, he thought.

Chapter 67

CALLAHAN HAD BEEN SO circumspect in his phone call that Dempsey wasn't at all sure what he had told him. However, the urgency of the message was completely comprehensible. Callahan wanted Dempsey to come to the island as quickly as possible; he would explain the situation in detail when he arrived.

Callahan waited for Dempsey at the ferry dock and greeted him with no more than a curt *Good to see you* before escorting him to the cruiser. He said nothing as they drove out of town and turned on to the coast road. Dempsey broke the silence.

"We're not going to the station?" he said.

"No," said Callahan. "We're stopping up ahead. We're almost there."

Dempsey looked up the road and saw nothing but a green stretch of woods on either side punctuated by mailboxes on posts and signs such a *Val's Halla, Haverford's Heaven,* and *Serenity Shores* revealing the entrance drives to secluded vacation homes. "Are we going to someone's house?" he asked.

Callahan just shook his head and then slowed, turned onto an unmarked dirt road, and stopped. "We get out here." He put his cell phone on the cruiser's center console and then opened the door. "Leave yours on the seat," he said, pointing to his phone.

Callahan led Dempsey to where the dirt road dwindled into a path. The short path ended at a picnic table in front of a split rail fence that marked an overlook to a lake vista. "Have a seat," he said.

Dempsey sat down. "What's going on, Matt?"

"This," he said, sitting down and handing Dempsey Nick's flash drive. "Nick found this. He'd forgotten he had it. It contains some of the data from the hard drive we found. Not all but a lot. I want you to have the data decrypted and tell me the results. Then return the flash drive to me. However, don't call me, text me, email me, or communicate with me in any way but in person, here on the island, and in a place of my choosing."

"Why all this cloak-and-dagger secrecy?" ask Dempsey.

"I believe that my office and phone may be bugged and my Wi-Fi and computers hacked. Whoever kidnapped Max knew where I had put the hard drive and when I was away from the station and Julie could be there alone. They even knew there were two flash drives with the hard drive. I want whatever is on this flash drive only to be between the two of us."

"I can have your office, phone, and computers swept clean by a team from Detroit. That would take care of the problem," said Dempsey. "There'd be no further need for all this rigmarole."

"No," said Callahan. "I want everything left as is."

Dempsey eyed Callahan as if he were a magician about to perform a card trick. "What have you got up your sleeve, Matt?" he said.

Chapter 68

A T MAX'S URGING, CALLAHAN hurled the frisbee as hard as he could; and he and Julie watched it sail down the beach as the dog and Max tore after it. They all had decided to have a walk together before dinner and chose the state forest trail down the road from the house that meandered to a strip of beach.

Again, the dog and Max were inseparable, each so aware of the other's presence that, like a pair of Olympic figure skaters, they moved in unison as a single organism. And their emotions didn't mirror each other's as much as spring from a single source. Julie marveled at the effect the dog was having on Max. He slept soundly, the dog at his feet on the bed. He smiled more, running with the dog on the beach or tossing a Frisbee into the surf and stomping after it with the dog to see who got to it first. Max never won, and that was fine with him. And Max was laughing again, big belly laughs when the dog would steal bacon from Callahan's breakfast plate and drop it in Max's lap under the table.

And the dog knew even before Max did when a dark memory of the kidnapping began to crystalize in Max's mind. It would leap up until his snout was in Max's face and push on Max's chest with its paws, almost knocking Max backwards and refocusing his attention on the present. The dog was a godsend, and thanks to it, Julie had felt that Max could to return to his job at the Adult Day Care Center. But she worried about their separation and considered asking the Center if the dog could be with Max at his job. Things were going so well for her and Max on the island that it shocked her when Callahan proposed she and Max visit her cousin in Ann Arbor.

"But why, Matt?"

The dog returned with the frisbee and circled the two of them before dropping it at Callahan's feet. Callahan picked it up and tossed it over Max's head. The dog scampered past Max and leaped to catch it before it floated to the ground.

"It'll just be for a few days, a week maybe. I can't tell you why, except I want you and Max safe; and I need to have my mind free of worry about the two of you," he said.

"What's going on? If you're worried about Max and me, then you might be in danger; and you think we will be too. If that's true, I need to know it. You can't keep me in the dark. Not after what's happened."

Callahan stopped walking and let Max and the dog get farther up the beach. "Okay. I haven't said anything to you because I believe our office is bugged and maybe our house too."

"What?" said Julie. "Who, why?"

"Just hear me out. Before Volkov died out on the lake, he said something to me and Amanda. He said he was going to use the hard drive we found to lure Susan Gibbons' killers out into the open.

Nick found a flash drive that he'd forgotten he'd used to transfer data from the hard drive. I want to use that flash drive as bait to lure the killers to me."

"No, Matt. No. It's too dangerous. Look how many people have already died. Volkov was a professional killer, and they were still able to kill him. I can't lose you. I won't." Julie's voice had risen to a shout, and Max and the dog had turned and were looking at her and Callahan.

"Calm down. Please," he said. He grabbed her shoulders and pulled her to his chest, hugging her tightly. "I don't want to lose you either or Max. I've thought this through. Amanda and I will have all the help we need from Dempsey and his agents. It has to be done. And you can help me most by taking Max and yourself to your cousin's. Take the dog too."

Julie pushed herself out of Callahan's arms and turned away from him. "It's never going to end is it, Matt? This worry and fear," she said.

Chapter 69

❧

"THE DATA FROM THE hard drive were encrypted twice—an encryption of an encryption, a double layer—and the original encryption was of Arabic. That's why it took a while for the team in Quantico to unravel all the data, but it did. And they caused quite a stir at headquarters in DC and at Justice. The data had to be analyzed and interpreted, their impact assessed, and their value determined. I didn't get back to you sooner because I had to be briefed on it all." Dempsey leaned back from the picnic table and twisted his torso so that he could look over the split-rail fence and survey the lake. "I like it here. It's secluded and peaceful, and the view's terrific."

Callahan chuffed in exasperation. "Well, go on. What did the data say? What was on the hard drive?"

Dempsey turned back to face Callahan. "The data on the flash drive were incomplete and fragmented, but, in a nutshell, here's what our analysts were able to piece together: It appears that money from three banks in Dubai was being funneled through Bland's corporation and philanthropical foundations to certain associations, political action groups, and election campaigns. It also appears that eight individuals benefited from these payouts: the governor of Michigan and seven senior members of the Michigan legislature. For example, key projects in their constituencies were funded, campaign coffers filled, and travel financed." Dempsey paused.

"So, money was being laundered," said Callahan.

"I said it *appears* that money was being funneled through Bland's company. We can't prove it was being laundered, not yet. Bland's company makes billions, and the way the money flows into and out of the company makes it a perfect vehicle for laundering. It buys startups. Then it rebrands them as its own, resells them, or strips the technology and improves it through research and development. His company also repurposes and sells the improved technology. Or it buys and kills startups that look as if they will compete successfully with products owned by Bland. Companies in Dubai may be legitimately purchasing his products or financing his research. The United Arab Emirates is big into technology.

"The payouts from Bland's company and foundations also appear legitimate." Dempsey shrugged. "But I think not. The eight individuals have one important thing in common: they're all vigorous proponents of legislation approving drilling for oil and natural gas in Lake Michigan. If we add into the mix the UAE's interest in investing in foreign oil production, then we may be looking at money laundering, mail fraud, and banking fraud to conceal the manipulation of a state legislature by a foreign individual or government. But to prove that, we would have to get legal authority to trace the money and invade the records of foreign and domestic financial institutions, corporations, and individuals. Do you know what it would take to do that?" The question was obviously rhetorical, so Callahan didn't respond.

Dempsey dangled the flash drive over the table and then cupped it in his hand. "This alone would not be enough to get us through the door," he said.

Callahan shook his head. "But none of this tells us who killed Susan Gibbons or Jackson," he said.

"No, it doesn't," said Dempsey, but he hesitated long enough before responding to signal indecision.

Callahan picked up on it. "There's something you're not telling me. Something you think I should know. What is it?" he demanded.

Dempsey took a deep breath and exhaled slowly. "What I'm going to tell you is highly confidential. Do not share it with anyone. Lives as well as the eventual success of a major criminal investigation depend on your silence. You understand. Right?" Callahan nodded, and Dempsey continued. "We learned through Susan Gibbons that money from her arm of the Thailand human-trafficking trade was being deposited in banks in Dubai. That wasn't surprising. The human-trafficking trade is huge and snakes far beyond Thailand, including into the US and other major countries. And most of the money from the trade is deposited in Dubai, which is the hub for the flow of that money. We're talking vast sums—almost unimaginable. However, through her testimony and other evidence, we were able to identify specific banks in Dubai. They're the ones on the flash drive. But we don't have enough evidence to establish a strong probability that the money from those banks is money from the trade that is being laundered, especially now that Gibbons is dead. Unfortunately, the data on the flash drive are missing that information."

"What sort of evidence would you need?" asked Callahan.

"It's not a stretch to imagine that Gibbons knew what was on the computer when she took it. That means she knew who possessed the computer or had access to the information on it. If she were alive, she could tell us who that was. That's the person we need to identify in order to make the connections we need. But without Gibbons . . . " Dempsey didn't finish his thought, but instead, dropped the flash drive on the table as if tossing away an extinguished match.

Callahan reached for the flash drive and picked it up. "That's who killed Susan Gibbons, had Jackson murdered, and Max kidnapped," Callahan said. "I think I know how to find that person."

Chapter 70

A SIMPLE PLAN CALLAHAN had said and explained. Whoever bugged his office and phone might still be listening. For their benefit, he would stage receiving from Nick the flash drive. He would then call Dempsey with the discovery. Dempsey would feign recognizing its importance and propose flying out to the island to retrieve it. Callahan would drive from the station to the airport to deliver the flash drive to Dempsey when he landed. The attempt to grab the bait would happen between the station and the airport. They would be ready for whomever the bait lured. Simple. Except that in Dempsey's experience, simple plans got complicated fast. Despite his reservations, he had pressed hard for approval to use his agents in executing Callahan's plan. He was now back on the island with the result.

Dempsey faced Callahan over the picnic table with the look of a bearer of bad news, which he was. "The Detroit office won't approve such an operation. I even took it up to the bureau in DC. Still a no-go. It's just too damn dangerous, Matt. You must know that," he said.

"How's it any different from a raid? You conduct them all the time, and they can be just as dangerous," said Callahan.

"Look, in a raid we know who the targets are. We can pick the place and the time. We can determine how the raid will be carried out to minimize the possibility of injury to our agents or to innocent bystanders. We're prepared and in control. What you're suggesting is totally out of control. We don't know who the targets are; where, when, and how they may choose to strike; and how we should respond. It's a hair's breadth shy of suicide."

"It's the only way to wrench them into the open. If we don't do this, they'll stay immune from capture. We might never get them," argued Callahan.

"Maybe, maybe not. If we keep digging for evidence, we may unearth enough to nail them."

"That's not going to happen unless you trace the money, and you don't have enough evidence to get authority for that. Even if you did, we're talking about money laundering and financial fraud, not murder."

Dempsey shrugged his shoulders and spread his arms as a silent signal that there was nothing more he could do.

"Pete, I'm after them for murder; and I'm going to get them with or without your help," said Callahan.

Dempsey rose from the picnic table and walked over to the split-rail fence. He leaned over it and looked down to the beach for a moment before turning around. The muscles in his face were taught and had hardened his features. "Don't do this, Matt. Please," he said.

* * *

Dempsey avoided the deck of the ferry and chose an interior seat in the lower lounge area. Only two passengers occupied seats, and

Dempsey quickly realized why. The low glass windows that stretched along both sides of the lounge didn't provide the open view of the water that the upper deck benches did. And even opened, the windows struggled to ventilate the lounge with the cool air that swept over the ferry. Instead, the mechanical clatter of three vending machines and the incessant clanging of the metal doors to the two lavatories filled the room. But none of this mattered to him. He wanted the solitude.

He pushed his back against the faux-leather chair until it reclined to the angle he wanted and tried to relax. The gentle vibration and the rising and falling thrum of the engines as they pushed the boat up and glided it down the swells helped. He was soon lulled into a mild trance where his thoughts mingled, tangling in random jumbles until they spun a single thread.

He envied Callahan the freedom he had to act unfettered by artificial restraints. Callahan's role as sheriff enabled him to exercise independent judgement, be proactive, and operate expeditiously. Next to Callahan, Dempsey felt professionally impotent. As he rose in the bureau, he faced an increasing mass of rules: often contradictory, never discretionary, always confining. The mass grew and menaced his authority until his judgement became infested with debilitating constraints, until his decisions twisted to avoid punitive consequences, until his leadership dwindled into micromanagement, until the only way he played it was safe, until he lost sight of who he was—a predator who needed to be in search of its prey.

The ferry passed its sister ship carrying passengers to the island, and both boats sounded a triple blast from their horns as a *hello* to each other. Dempsey sat up and watched from the window as the other ship glided by in the opposite direction, passengers waving from the decks. His mind had settled, the turmoil congealing into a rock-hard resolution. He would not abandon Callahan. If he could not employ the resources of the bureau, then he would go it alone, even if it meant his career. He would be the hunter again.

Chapter 71

NICK HAD PERFORMED HIS part well, again presenting Callahan with the newly discovered flash drive. This time the performance took place in Callahan's office, and this time included Nick's claim that the drive contained *most* of the data from the hard drive. Callahan had credibly feigned surprise and excitement and had called Dempsey from his office with the news. Dempsey had played his role like a noted thespian, immediately recognizing its importance as evidence and stressing the need to preserve an unassailable chain of custody. He didn't want to risk receiving it by mail or messenger. He would fly to the island to pick it up personally—tomorrow. He would call back when he had scheduled the flight. When he did, Callahan would tell him that he would be waiting for him at the airport with the flash drive.

Callahan hoped that the charade had accomplished two things: revealing the bait and accelerating the reaction time. He wanted whoever was coming for him and the flash drive to have no time to prepare properly. They would have to wing it: off balance, unsuspecting, and vulnerable. That was the plan anyway. He also hoped that they'd been listening. It all depended on that.

*   *   *

Amanda unfolded the map and spread it on the metal table. She and Callahan had driven to the small park beside the marina. Callahan chose the spot because it was uncrowded but had enough ambient noise to ensure that their conversation would be undetected. She bent over the map and traced west with her finger along the road out of town to Sutter Road and then south until she reached its intersection with Millrace Road. "You're pretty much okay until here," she said, keeping her finger on the intersection. "Mostly open grassy fields and farms until you hit the state forest at this intersection. The road to the airport goes through it. The road is gravel so you're going to have to go slow. You're an easy moving target then for anyone with a rifle hiding in the woods. You won't be able to see them. You'd be a sitting duck." She'd been trying for days to discourage Callahan from this gamble, ever since he had told her of it. He'd simply ignored her, just like he was ignoring her warnings now.

Callahan stood next to Amanda, stooped over the map at almost her level. He turned his head toward her. "They're going to ambush the cruiser, make sure I have the flash drive, and then authenticate it. If it's not real, they'll want to know where the real one is. They need me alive for that. So, I want your help in figuring out where that's most likely to happen," he said. "Now where do you think they'll show up?"

"According to our plan, Dempsey is scheduled to take the first flight from Charlevoix to the island. He won't be on that flight of course. He'll already be here on the island with us. That will be early in the morning, and there'll be almost no traffic to and from the center of the island where the airport is. It's pretty isolated there, just the two airport runways and a couple of farms. You could be the only car on Millrace Road at that time. I'd say it's going to happen here." Amanda pointed to where Millrace Road took a sharp bend south and then curved back west. "When you make the turn here, you have to slow way down; and you're invisible to any traffic coming from both the east and west. If they can somehow stop you there, they can grab the flash drive and get off the island fast."

"How can they do that? They're in the middle of the island on the only road there," said Callahan.

"Do you see this trail?" Amanda put her finger on a faint dotted line that began just off the road at the beginning of the curve and meandered northwest to a point about a half mile from the shore.

"Yes," said Callahan.

"And do you see where it ends?"

"Yes again," said Callahan.

"That trail ends on Egan's property right where that oil rig is being dismantled by Superior Tow and Salvage. Its helicopter is loading the parts onto the barge moored in Pebble Bay. If they had a waiting ATV, they could make it up the trail to the helicopter and be off the island in no time. I think there'll be three of them, and I think that's how they intend to do it," said Amanda.

Callahan straightened up and emitted a low whistle until his breath was gone. "Damn," he said.

Chapter 72

❀

SURPRISE AND TIMING. HE had those two elements on his side. Callahan was reasonably certain that whoever would come for him did not know he knew his office was bugged. They would not know he had prepared for them. They also had to anticipate his schedule. He was in control of the timing.

Amanda would be hidden on the trail. Dempsey would be waiting at the well rig. If he and Amanda failed to seize them, then it would be up to Dempsey. There would be no communication between the three of them, nothing to nullify the element of surprise, until Callahan was in sight of them and the attackers had made their move.

Callahan pulled the seatbelt across his chest and fastened it. The flash drive was in a padded envelope in the glove compartment. He backed the cruiser out of the station's driveway and rolled onto the road. He headed west.

Callahan drove through town to its western edge where the road rose in a gentle incline for a mile to a crest where it intersected with

Sutter Road. He had an unobstructed view, and not a single car came over the crest toward him or came up the incline behind him. The road remained clear all the way to the intersection. At the intersection, he turned south onto Sutter Road. It lay straight as an arrow for three miles until it formed a tee with Millrace Road at the state forest. There he would turn west again and into the suspected trap.

The geography was as Amanda had described it, flat open fields and farms and barren shoulders edging the road on either side. The day had started to heat up, and the asphalt road began to shimmer ahead of the cruiser. Just inside the shimmer, he could see two cars in his lane. Both were close together and going slower than the speed limit. When he closed the distance between the cruiser and the first car ahead of him, he signaled to pass. As he turned into the oncoming lane, the first car slammed on its brakes and the second car plowed into its rear with an impact so great that the cruiser shook. He saw the airbags explode and the interior of both cars swirl with white dust. Callahan hit the brakes and rumbled to the side of the road. As he jumped from the cruiser, the driver's-side door of the second car opened and a woman staggered out. She lunged for the rear door and jerked on the handle, struggling to open it. She began to scream. "My baby, my baby. Please, someone help. My baby." The driver's door to the first car opened and another woman tumbled out onto the road and tried to push herself to her knees, her head dangling to her chest.

Callahan rushed to the first woman and wrenched the rear door open. He saw the baby in a rear-facing infant car seat covered in a blanket. He ducked into the car, reached over the car seat, unfastened the seat belt, and tore the blanket off the child. Then he froze.

*   *   *

Amanda hadn't moved a muscle in over an hour. She had selected a hiding spot that commanded a view of the trail head and that was high enough to see the road. Then she made herself invisible. She had done this dozens of times before in blinds, tower stands, and the open forest. Her brother had taught her to hunt and shoot a rifle. Once she learned, she never missed a kill shot. Some of the happiest times of her life had been hunting with her brother. She thought of him now and how proud of her he would be for choosing to be a deputy sheriff. She missed him terribly. No one could stop him from joining the army, training for the military police, and volunteering for deployment to a war zone. The last time she saw him alive he was in his uniform. He was in his same uniform when they buried him. Her brother's influence and example had kindled in her a fierce desire to serve in law enforcement.

She was good for several more hours, no problem; but she worried. Callahan should have passed the trail head by now, and she had seen no sign of anyone on the trail. Something went wrong. She had hidden her car off the road a half mile away. If she ran to it, she could be there in minutes, cruising the roads toward town that Callahan would follow to the airport. She waited five more minutes and then stood up out of the brush. Callahan wasn't coming.

Amanda sprinted to her car and fifteen minutes later stopped on the side of the road opposite the two wrecked automobiles. So that was it. Callahan had come upon the accident and either called an ambulance or taken the injured to the emergency medical facility himself. He had of necessity abandoned their plan. She sighed with relief and silently prayed for anyone who may have been hurt.

*   *   *

Callahan backed away from the plastic doll in the car seat and felt something blunt and hard bore into his spine. "Get out of the car slowly and start walking to your vehicle. Don't turn around. You try to be a hero, and I blow a hole in your back, a big one." The woman had stopped screaming and now her voice sounded low and hard.

"God damn you." It was a second female voice. "My fucking teeth are broken and maybe my nose." Callahan heard her spit. "You were supposed to slow down before you hit me, bitch."

"It's your own damn fault. You stopped too fast," said the first woman. "Have you got the computer and phone?"

"Hell yes," said the second woman and spat again.

Callahan's head cleared the ceiling of the car, and he stood up, facing over the roof.

"Put your hands on your head," said the first woman. When Callahan complied, she barked to the second woman, "Get his gun and then get into the cruiser. Hurry."

*   *   *

Amanda traveled a short distance down the road when she made a U-turn and headed back to the accident. She'd make a quick inspection of the site and take a few pictures before meeting up with Callahan at the medical facility. Her training demanded it.

The rear of the first car had folded like an accordion. The bumper dangled from the chassis, held there by a twisted strand of plastic. The left rear tire was flat, and the wheel broken from the axel. The driver's air bag had deployed and was spotted with thick smudges of blood-filled dust. Someone had been injured.

The second car's hood had popped open, the bumper and grill crushed. Oil floated over a large pool of liquid under the engine. Inside, the driver's air bag had also deployed, but there were no signs of an injury to the driver. The rear passenger door lay open and when Amanda inspected the back seat, her heart sank. A doll sat in a child's seat. A child must have been a passenger and the door opened to take it from the car. She hoped against hope that the abandoned doll was not a sign the child had been hurt.

As she turned to leave, she noticed a dull glint from an object on the floor. She thought it must be a baby toy of some kind knocked form the child's hand by the collision. She bent down to pick it up. When she pulled her hand out of the shadow and into full light, she was holding Callahan's sheriff's badge.

Chapter 73

THE FIRST WOMAN TWISTED toward Callahan, her back propped against the door, her left leg lying bent on the seat. She pointed the gun at Callahan as he drove.

"Keep your eyes on the road and drive where I tell you," she said.

He'd gotten a solid glimpse of her when she climbed into the passenger seat: early thirties, thin but taught, muscular. She wore shorts and a loose long-sleeved t-shirt. He suspected she hid tattoos. Her pale blue baseball cap covered all but a few strands of brown hair. He'd stolen another glance at her when she'd opened the glove compartment and tossed the envelope with the flash drive to the second woman in the back seat.

Except for the confusion in the seconds following the wreck, he'd not had an opportunity to observe the second woman. The first woman had rotated the rearview mirror so that he couldn't see into the back seat. He'd heard the second woman speak when she had cursed the first woman. She talked faster and sounded younger, her voice oddly rising and falling with the last words of a sentence. Since entering the cruiser, she had spoken just one word, *Done*, in a phone call that lasted a fraction of a second. Now she was speaking again.

"Fuck, fuck, FUCK! We don't have a goddamn cell signal. We've lost it. What's with this fucking island that you can't get a fucking signal?"

"The cell phone signal is too weak here. Where is it stronger?" The first woman spoke to Callahan.

"If you need a consistent signal, we have to get closer to town. That won't happen unless we turn around. If we keep going in this direction, it will just get weaker," he said.

"Turn this car around," the first woman said to Callahan. "Let me know when the signal is strong enough," she said to the second woman.

"I've downloaded the drive. I just need a minute to send the file. Then we wait until we get confirmation it's the real deal. After that, we get off this fucking island, and I punch you in the goddamn face for breaking my teeth," said the second woman.

Callahan turned the cruiser around and drove toward town. He was as determined as the two women to get to a stronger signal.

*   *   *

Dempsey had purchased the hard hat at the hardware store and the ancient Carhartt work jacket at Goodwill. The clipboard had come from the grocery store's school supplies section. Like his disguise, his heads-up, in-charge demeanor was fabricated. He felt conspicuously out of place; yet, it all seemed to be working. So far, two workers at the drill site had approached him thinking he was a supervisor. But he didn't know how much longer he could hang around before someone suspected that he didn't belong there. He'd been waiting a long time, too long. He was supposed to be the fallback guy. If Callahan's plan backfired, then he was there to stop anyone from escaping the island by helicopter. The helicopter had not landed to pick anyone up. And no one had come or gone from the rig site. Maybe the plan had worked. But why hadn't Callahan contacted him? Something had gone wrong. He was sure of it.

He heard the car before he saw it—the piercing growl of an engine under stress and the hollow thuds of a two-ton metallic mass. When he turned toward the din, he saw a car racing down the dirt road to the site, swerving in the ruts and pounding over its pitted surface, heedless of obstacles. It skidded to a stop just feet from the well's perimeter barricade causing two workers to backpedal away from the chain-link fence. The door flung open, and a woman jumped out, frantically waving her arms above her head.

It took Dempsey a few seconds to comprehend the scene and realize what was happening. The woman was Amanda and she was waving at him.

*   *   *

"I've got a signal. Stop the car," demanded the second woman. The first woman waved the muzzle of the gun toward the side of the road for Callahan to pull over and stop.

This was the moment Callahan had been waiting for. Once the file was sent, the computer in the second woman's hands would contain the identity of the receiving computer. With that identity, its location could be determined. And that location would reveal who had been behind the murders and kidnapping. Callahan had to get the computer from the women and get it to Dempsey. His window of opportunity would slam shut when they received the reply that the data were authentic. Then they would kill him, destroy the computer and flash drive, and bolt from the island.

"Come on, come on, come on," urged the second woman. "Bingo. They got it and its good," she cheered in the second before she screamed.

*   *   *

"Callahan never got to the trail. When I backtracked on the road, I passed an accident: two cars, no one at the scene, evidence of an injury, and this on the floor of one of the cars." She reached into her pocket and tossed Dempsey the badge. "It's Callahan's."

"So they got him," he said.

"I called the medical facility. No one was admitted who needed medical attention, and the EMTs weren't dispatched to any accident.

"Do you know where they might have taken him?"

Amanda shook her head. She drove toward town away from the drill site. If the abductors were on their way to the helicopter, she and Dempsey would meet them. The road wasn't safe above 30 mph, and she was doing 70 when the tractor pulled onto the road in front of them. She slammed on the brakes and jerked the wheel to the left. The car fishtailed and then skidded broadside on the gravel before spinning to a stop across both lanes of traffic just in front of the tractor, missing it by feet.

The tractor had stopped, and the driver climbed down from the seat. Amanda pushed open the car door. Dempsey was already out of the vehicle. That's when they heard the siren.

Chapter 74

CALLAHAN SAT WITH HIS arms at his side and his head tilted back against the headrest watching the first woman out of the corner of his eye. She was still turned sideways, her back leaning against the door, her left leg bent and propped against the backrest of the front seat. She held the gun easily in her right hand close to her chest, her elbow tucked at her side. The muzzle pointed at Callahan's heart, and neither it nor the woman's eyes had shifted away from Callahan for even a second. Callahan hadn't moved or spoken since he stopped the cruiser. His breathing had settled into a steady rhythm as he waited, his hand inches from the siren button on the center console. The sound he waited for was maybe moments away and when it came, he would take his chance. He fought against his body's urge to tense. He struggled to keep his muscles relaxed and his breathing even.

Then it happened.

There was a clap when the second woman slapped shut the computer. In that instant, Callahan jammed the button, and the siren blasted. Both women jumped, startled. And Callahan spun, grabbed the second woman's hair with his right hand and slammed her face against the top of the seat. With his left hand, he seized the first woman's gun and twisted it a full 360 degrees. The woman's wrist cracked, and her forefinger snapped in half as the gun fired into the console. Still griping the second woman's hair, he wrenched a fistful from her scalp and threw himself across the front seat, smashing his forehead into the first woman's face, breaking her nose. Both women's screams hovered above the wail of the siren. Jerking the gun from the first woman's hand, Callahan swung it at the second woman just as she lifted her gun above the backrest.

The windshield shattered, and the first woman's head exploded, hurling bone fragments into the face and neck of the second woman whose screams ceased as she teetered sideways and slumped onto the rear seat.

Dempsey stood at the hood of the cruiser, aiming his gun through the windshield. Amanda, gun drawn, opened the passenger-side door, and the first woman's body careened backwards and tumbled to the ground.

The siren moaned into silence and Dempsey lowered his gun. "Holy shit," he said. "Talk about mayhem."

Chapter 75

A MANDA HAD ERECTED MAKESHIFT traffic barriers blocking any oncoming traffic from passing the cruiser. So far, she had directed only a few cars to turn around and head away from the scene. But that was enough for Callahan.

"It's only going to be minutes before this goes viral on social media and less than an hour before it appears online in the *Ledger*. Gallagher probably is already on his way over here. Whoever hired these two is going to find out what happened to them very soon," said Callahan. Already, he could hear the ambulance sirens.

Dempsey was holding the computer. "It's going to take at least 24 hours to get this analyzed," he said.

"Then we're going to lose them. That's more time than they need to erase their digital footprints," said Callahan.

"What about the phone? Did she use it?" Amanda was standing at the open door of the cruiser and pointing to the dead woman slumped across the back seat. The woman wore tight jeans and the conspicuous bulge in her rear pocket conformed to the contours of a cell phone.

"She did," said Callahan. He leaned into the back of the cruiser and removed the phone from the second woman's pocket. He pushed himself back out, and while Dempsey and Amanda looked over his shoulder, he searched it for the most recent numbers dialed. There was only one. "Can you trace this call and find the phone?" Callahan asked Dempsey.

"If the other phone still exists and is on, I can. All I need to do is give the Detroit office that number. I'm sure both phones are burners and are meant to be destroyed. But if another call was supposed to be made, then they may be waiting for it and we're in luck." Dempsey snapped his phone out of its case on his belt and began dialing.

*   *   *

The return call from Detroit came within minutes, but the wait seemed like an hour to the three of them. Dempsey answered his phone when it vibrated before the first ring tone, listened for a moment, and then frantically gestured with his right hand for something to write with. Amanda handed Dempsey her pen, and then took her notepad from her shirt pocket and held it open in front of him. He scribbled something on the page, grabbed the pad, and then ended the call.

"The phone is near the island, sort of. I wrote down the coordinates. But according to the office, its geolocation put it out in the lake and then it disappeared," said Dempsey. He shook his head. "Something must be wrong."

"There's nothing wrong," said Amanda. "They're on a boat. Show me those coordinates."

*   *   *

Amanda pushed the Vigilant into a headwind that raised a chop on the lake, and the boat began to slap the waves and throw up a spray when she increased its speed. Callahan and Dempsey huddled behind the wheelhouse to keep dry and held tight to whatever they could while the boat bucked over the chop. The wind turned cool and bit through their clothing as the bay disappeared behind them and they shot into open water.

Amanda handed Callahan the binoculars. "We're about ten minutes from where the coordinates placed the phone. See what you can find out there," she shouted over the thunder of the engines.

Callahan scanned the water, holding the binoculars in one hand. Nothing. The strong wind would discourage leisure boaters, both sail and motor, from venturing far from shore, and as Amanda charged closer to the point of the coordinates, he saw nothing but empty lake.

"We just passed through the phone's last location," yelled Amanda. She pointed ahead of her to Eagle Island, the closest outer island to them. "I'm going to circle the island and see if anyone's there. It's about three miles away."

Callahan nodded, and Dempsey gave a thumbs-up.

As they approached the lee of the island, the wind calmed; and Amanda slowed the boat. She stayed well off shore to avoid a forested point that projected from the center of the island into the water almost a half mile. When the Vigilant cleared the point, the *Odyssey* came into view. It was anchored off a pristine beach where open tents had been erected, tables set, and a buffet banquet spread for the two dozen guests who swam, sunned, and dined along the salt-white sand. On the *Odyssey*, Bland stepped away from the taffrail and crossed the deck, entering a cabin.

Chapter 76

✪

AT HOME, CALLAHAN LEANED against the kitchen sink and unbuttoned the top two buttons of his shirt. He pulled it over his head and tossed it into the trashcan by the dishwasher. It was blood-splattered, and he didn't want Julie to see it. He would burn it with other waste in the barrel behind the cabin before she returned with Max from her cousin's.

He filled a glass with water from the tap and drank without pause until it was empty. He placed the glass in the sink and then walked to the bathroom where he turned on the shower full blast and waited for the water to heat. He couldn't avoid the large wall mirror, so succumbed and looked at himself full on. His mask was cracked and chipped, and an ugly bruise spread across his forehead. He had deep scratches on his neck, and blood flecked his hair. His eyes looked haunted.

Julie had asked if this would ever end. The visage in the mirror that stared back at him answered her question. He could no longer meet the toll demanded by this case. It was all too much: the lives lost and taken, the blood spilled, the psychological devastation, its reach encircling those closest to him. And still Susan Gibbons' and Jackson's killers eluded him. He wanted it over. He wanted it to end, now.

The mirror began to fog, and as the room filled with steam from the shower, the fog grew thicker until his image receded far into the mist.

Chapter 77

@/@

UNTIL NOW, GALLAGHER'S HOPED-for career as a muckraker had faltered. His forays into investigative journalism involved skimming the thin layer of scum on the surface of small ponds of corruption. The filth he discovered was microscopic and rarely newsworthy. The real dirt lurked deep under the surface, buried under layers of mud, out of his reach. But not anymore, thanks to Callahan. Callahan's landing on the island had been a godsend to the *Ledger*. To Gallagher, Callahan was like a whirlpool churning the water and spinning faster and deeper until it roiled the mud, releasing all it had concealed. What rose to the surface and washed ashore was sometimes journalistic treasure. And Gallagher had just salvaged one such prize.

As part of his exposé on Deep Sea Gas and Petroleum and its secret drilling on the lake, he had written background on Infinity Cyber and Bland, which included a description and picture of Bland's mega yacht. Apparently, someone had read it. He had received a call from a crew member of the barge tug that had ferried the components of the oil rig to Tom Egan's property. The tug had been on a night run when the crew member spotted a large boat on the radar screen.

As the tug got closer, a yacht loomed out of the darkness of the lake. The two ships passed within a half mile of each other, and the crew member had observed the yacht through binoculars. He saw something thrown or fall overboard from an upper deck. The yacht had immediately slowed and conducted a 180 degree turn. Two powerful search lights swept the water until the beams converged on the surface ahead of the yacht. It had then increased its speed and passed over the spot. It sailed away without stopping.

The scene had been so unusual that it stuck in the crew member's memory, and when he had read Gallagher's article in the *Ledger,* he recognized the *Odyssey.* He also heard about the body of the girl being found on the beach and its condition. He put two and two together and called Gallagher. When Gallagher asked why he hadn't called the police, he answered that the police knew him, and he wanted to stay clear of law enforcement. He also did not want to get into any trouble with his employer, Superior Tow and Salvage. He demanded to be an anonymous source and did not ask for money before giving Gallagher the details of his story. He just thought he should come forward with what he knew.

A reclusive billionaire tied to the gruesome death of a young woman was big news, and Gallagher was determined to pursue it. He called Bland with the story to get his response. Bland had said that nothing of the sort had ever happened and threatened to sue Gallagher and the *Ledger* for libel if he reported such garbage or implied that his yacht had killed the girl found on the beach. Gallagher then contacted Callahan to see what he knew about any connection between Bland's yacht and the death of Susan Gibbons.

Chapter 78

ᎧᎧ

"THERE ISN'T ANY CONNECTION, and even if there was, you know damn well I can't comment on an ongoing investigation."

Callahan and Gallagher stood shoulder to shoulder on the dock watching the sheriff's cruiser being loaded onto the ferry. It was being sent to the mainland for repair.

"C'mon Callahan. You have screwed the lid down so tight on the investigation of Gibbons' death that it has to mean something big is up. Shit, the body count on this island is higher than Beirut; the FBI is swarming all over the place; and you're making it seem like a liquor store robbery. It all must be connected," said Gallagher.

"No comment," said Callahan.

"Bullshit. Don't give me that. You're protecting Bland. That's it, isn't it? He's involved in this, and he's got enough money and influence to shut everybody up."

Callahan turned so quickly toward Gallagher that he jerked back and raised both hands in front of him.

"You'd better be damned careful what you say, write, or even think unless you can substantiate it," said Callahan.

Gallagher dropped his hands but kept his distance from Callahan. "It's not just me. It's what everyone is going to think," he said.

"What do you mean *going to think*? What have you got on Bland?" said Callahan.

"You know how this works," said Gallagher. "Tit for tat. You scratch my back; I'll scratch yours. Quid pro quo. Need I go on?"

Gallagher had seen the look Callahan gave him often enough to fathom what was behind the veneer of disgust. "You first," he said.

Callahan weighed the options and decided it was worth giving Gallagher the bones of his investigation to find out what he knew. He took a deep breath. "Susan Gibbons was hired as a nanny for the children of guests on the *Odyssey*. She would have been on the yacht around the time of her death. A later examination of her body showed a pattern of abrasions on her legs that matched the safety netting on one of the yacht's decks. That's all I've got."

A slow smile boosted Gallagher's satisfied expression. "You're going to love what I'm about to tell you," he said.

Chapter 79

CALLAHAN LAY ON THE narrow beach along Mystic Point with his head propped on a towel and his cell phone resting on his chest. Dempsey had called earlier and requested that he leave the office and find a place to call back. He had something important to tell him and was still leery that the station was bugged. Callahan used the opportunity to go to a secluded beach and have a quick, refreshing swim before he got back to Dempsey. Gusts off the lake chilled him when he first got out of the water but had lost their effect as he reclined on the beach and his body absorbed the warmth of the sand. He watched clouds spilling over the horizon as Dempsey spoke.

"The two women who hijacked you were Cynthia Vaughn and Elizabeth Spacek, both convicted felons who freelanced together doing smash-and-grab jobs for different crime syndicates. We're doing a deep check on them, but so far, no leads on who hired them to grab you. That's the bad news. The good news is we've identified the computer they communicated with and pinpointed its geolocation."

"When you say *pinpoint*, how accurate do you mean?" asked Callahan.

"The accuracy is classified, but I can tell you that it was good enough to get permission to capture and examine the records of the financial institutions and individuals, foreign and domestic, necessary to follow the money. We're now getting the evidence to prove some heavy-duty financial crimes including bank fraud and money laundering. It also looks like a lot of the money wound up in the political coffers of seven state legislators plus the governor. Maybe even in their personal pockets. We're exploring that too. This is strictly confidential, but if the evidence shows that Abdullah and Bland colluded in a scheme to conceal the flow of foreign money into the U.S. to influence the outcome of a state's legislative process, then they both could wind up in prison. We owe you big time, Matt. That was a gutsy move, but it paid off handsomely," said Dempsey.

"Payback could be larger and come sooner than you think," said Callahan.

"What do you mean, Matt?" said Dempsey.

"Gibbons' and Jackson's murders are my top priority, not Bland's financial crimes. I may . . ." Just then a male swan emerged from behind a thick stand of bulrush along the shore and glided over to where Callahan lay. It began clacking its beak and emitting a stuttering hiss, demanding a handout. "Listen, send me what you've got on the women. I've got to go now. I'll be in touch," he said.

Chapter 80

NICK SAT ACROSS FROM Callahan in a booth at O'Malley's trying to hide his nervousness behind what he hoped was a casual smile and a laid-back posture. Instead, the smile felt like a satanic grin, and his posture had crumpled into a slump so low that his head floated just above the edge of the table. He was certain he looked like something out of a Stephen King novel. Callahan eyed him strangely, but he felt paralyzed. Amanda had tipped him off that Callahan wanted to meet with him about something important, but Callahan had been vague about what it was. They both hoped it involved a job offer down the line when he had passed his exams and qualified as a sheriff's deputy. That was months away, but, in the meantime, they figured he could find a temporary job on the mainland to hold things together until then. He crossed his fingers and peered over the edge of the table as Callahan spoke.

"Are you okay?" asked Callahan.

"What? I mean yes, sure, I'm fine," said Nick.

"Shall we order and eat first? You look like you might need some food, or are you good with getting down to business?" said Callahan. "This won't take long."

"No, no. Business is good. Let's go for it. I mean, I'm good with that. I mean, whatever you prefer I'm good with. I mean, it's all good," stammered Nick.

"Good," said Callahan, not without irony. "Okay then. As sheriff, Michigan law gives me the authority to appoint any person a deputy for a special purpose. That person is called a special deputy. The appointment must be in writing and specific." Callahan removed a sheet of paper from a manila folder beside him on the booth's bench. "I'm appointing you a special deputy for technology."

Nick suddenly sat bolt upright. He was stunned. This, he did not expect.

"Your training and experience with the NSA are invaluable to me," Callahan continued. "That being said, I can only pay you the starting salary of a deputy during the term of your appointment." Callahan shrugged and smiled. "Your first task is to debug the station. Your second but simultaneous task is to find out everything you can about the two women who hijacked me and, particularly, who hired them. Their names and what the FBI knows about them already are on this paper." Callahan handed the sheet to Nick. "You'll also have access to all law enforcement data bases such as the National Crime Information Center, the FBI's Combined DNA Index System, Homeland Security's Automated Targeting System, and so on. What do you say?"

"I . . . I . . . I . . . ," Nick sputtered.

"Great. That's settled. Time is of the essence, so I want you to get started immediately. I'm advancing you a month's pay. And you'll have a desk at the station if you need it. Here's a key." Callahan handed Nick a key on a ring. "Special deputies don't get a badge. Sorry. Now, what are you having to eat?" asked Callahan. "I'm starved."

Chapter 81

GALLAGHER HAD DECIDED ON another exposé. If Bland wanted to duck his inquiries into Susan Gibbons' death, then he would turn up the heat until the pot boiled. He'd get the big boys interested in Bland. The headline he just typed read:

RECLUSIVE ISLAND BILLIONAIRE
MUM ON DEATH OF EMPLOYEE

The article below it began with a slap at both Callahan and Bland:

The investigation into the suspicious death of young island resident and female employee of Anthony Bland, Susan Gibbons, goes nowhere as billionaire Bland shelters in his luxury bunker avoiding the press.

The rest of the article recounted what was known about Susan Gibbons' connections to Bland, her presence on his yacht, and local sightings of the yacht around the time of her death, including one from an anonymous source. It referenced the impotence of local law enforcement before it ended with a list of questions and a public plea for answers.

Gallagher radiated the smugness of a self-satisfied scoundrel. He would either get sued or get answers. Either way, the *Ledger* would profit from the publicity. Or so he thought. He wasn't prepared for Bland's comeback.

Chapter 82

۞

O'DONNELL HAD BEEN OVER the moon with gratitude when Bland left his office. His eyes glazed with amazement while he shook Bland's hand, pumping his arm wildly until Bland jerked free of his grip. Philanthropy (or *purchased prestige* as Bland preferred to call it) had that effect on people. And he was going to need all the prestige he could get. He sensed a shit storm of bad press coming, thanks to Gallagher, and he was working to head it off.

Bland donated the funds for a new playground and gym for the island's school and promised additional funds for a new library wing. He'd contacted his corporate media officer and ordered a media blitz touting his good deeds and portraying him as a benefactor of the island. He wanted Gallagher's stories washed away by a tsunami of shining press releases, planted news briefs, and public interest broadcasts. But his real strategy was to make Gallagher the story, to turn the tables on him.

Bland had some digging done and had struck a vein of gold. The *Ledger* and Gallagher had struggled financially for years. Gallagher owed a bundle in back real estate taxes and had a mountain of credit card debt. But the gold was that he had used money from his advertisers to pay his personal expenses. Gallagher covered it well but not well enough.

The first whiff that Gallagher cooked his books came when he applied for a business loan. He'd been honest about the *Ledger's* income and expenses on all the forms, but the bank had demanded that the loan be secured by Gallagher personally. That's where Gallagher had played with his income from the business. His finagling was minor but enough to put the bank on guard and cause the loan to be denied.

After that, Gallagher panicked. He needed money fast, and his misadventure with high finance grew darker. Gallagher was an amateur, and the scent was easy for Bland's bloodhounds to follow. Embezzlement and bank fraud were always big news.

*   *   *

Bland stretched out on the leather couch in the master suite of his yacht. The suite encompassed an entire upper deck, and the sweep of glass that surrounded the suite, plus its high vantage point created a cyclorama of the lake. The yacht cruised north, passing on the windward side of the outer islands known as the Three Sisters. Formed of rock sculpted by glacial erosion, they had risen close together above the meltwater. Wind and current extended their beaches so that they appeared to be reaching out to hold hands to keep one another from drifting apart. The main island floated behind them like a sheltering mother. Few would ever experience this perspective, but its drama was lost on Bland.

He had ended his call to Dubai, and as usual, his consultation with Abdullah proved informative. Abdullah counseled a lighter touch with Gallagher—a carrot and stick approach. Perhaps it was time that Bland's company acquired a media outlet or two. The *Ledger* could be a perfect acquisition considering Bland's investment in the island. The offer would be enticing enough to create visions of a quick and secure retirement for Gallagher that would not include prison time. Bland was sure it would work.

He dialed the number of his corporate finance officer. As he waited for the connection, he wondered if exorcizing Callahan from his life would be as easy.

Chapter 83

IT HADN'T TAKEN AMANDA long to find Danny Ayres. The manager of Superior Tow and Salvage's small office in Charlevoix immediately named the *Raggedy Anne's* three crew members and then checked her records to make sure the tug transported a barge to the island on the night the crew member sighted the *Odyssey*. It had. The *Raggedy Anne's* captain, Ed Bagley, had been on night duty for two weeks and was now home asleep. The engineer, Tom Sizemore, worked on another push boat currently out on the lake. Ayres, the deck hand that night, could be found in the dockyard.

The manager offered a detailed and unflattering description of Danny: a boney snot of a kid with dirty straw hair, a pinched face, baggy clothes, and an attitude. Danny leaned against a column of used tires in the dockyard smoking a cigarette when Amanda walked up to him, identified herself, and showed him her badge. He blew a cloud of smoke at her and then turned to the side and spit on the ground. "What do you want?" he asked. His voice was pitched to the edge of a whine.

"I want to ask you about the night the *Raggedy Anne* pushed a barge to the island and you saw something happen on the yacht *Odyssey.*"

"What? How did . . . He said that . . . Shit. Am I in trouble?" asked Danny.

"No, and you're not going to be in trouble. I just need answers to some questions about what you saw. That's all," said Amanda.

"I need this job. I don't want to lose it. I can't afford to," said Danny, the whine in his voice rising. "My girlfriend wants to get married," he added.

"You'll be fine. You won't lose your job. I'll make sure your employer knows you've done nothing wrong and aren't implicated in any way in any wrongdoing. You're just one of several people we're interviewing who may have witnessed something. We'll be interviewing the captain and engineer too. It's routine," said Amanda.

"I'm trying to change my life. My girlfriend said I should tell what I saw. That it was the right thing to do. I shouldn't have listened to her," said Danny, unconvinced.

"Your girlfriend was right, Danny. You should listen to her. Now please tell me what you saw that night. You'll be a better person for it, and your girlfriend will be proud of you," said Amanda.

Danny shook his head and Amanda thought he was refusing to talk. Then he said, "I don't need to tell you."

"It's true you don't have to answer my questions—" began Amanda, but Danny interrupted her.

"No, you don't understand. I don't need to tell you," said Danny, emphasizing the word *tell.*

"Why not?" asked Amanda, confused.

"Because I videoed everything. It's all on my smart phone," said Danny.

* * *

Danny had emailed the video to Amanda, and Callahan and Nick watched as she played it for them for the third time on her phone. Danny had a new, high-end, dual-camera phone with a telephoto zoom, not a digital zoom. His girlfriend gave it to him for his birthday, and he had started videoing the *Odyssey* to show her what life on the lake was like for him and how well the camera worked. When he showed the video to her, she was adamant—he had to tell someone about it.

The camera had worked very well. It captured and magnified the ambient light of the evening to illuminate the ship and surrounding water like early dusk. Danny had used the telephoto function for part of the video, which significantly enlarged the image without reducing the resolution. When the video started, the silhouettes of two people could be seen standing near the railing of an upper deck. From the size and shape of the shadows, one appeared to be a man and the other a woman. As the video played, the two began to struggle, and the woman fell overboard into the water. She disappeared before resurfacing behind the yacht. The man vanished from the deck, and the yacht slowed and began to make a turn. Searchlights scanned the water before converging on the woman who was swimming away from the yacht. The yacht then completed its turn, picked up speed, and churned over the spot where the lights had found her. The video ended there.

God bless that girlfriend, thought Callahan.

Chapter 84

ᘒᘒ

NICK SET THE BLUE index card on Callahan's desk and slid it toward Callahan.

"What's this?" Callahan looked up from the notes he was making and examined the card.

"These are the listening devices I found at the station," said Nick.

Callahan peered at the card again and then shrugged. "I don't see anything," he said

"Here, take a closer look," said Nick and handed him a small magnifying glass.

Callahan slowly moved the glass over the card. Barely visible were three strips of clear tape with what looked like a human hair attached to each. "How— " Callahan started to speak but Nick jumped in with the explanation Callahan wanted.

"I found them on the windows of the station. They were all but invisible. Each has a tiny chip—it's almost microscopic—with a super thin wire attached. That's the transmitter. The tape picks up vibrations from the window glass. When anyone talks in the station, the sound waves strike the glass causing it to vibrate. The vibrations are transmitted to a receiver somewhere outside the station. The receiver converts the vibrations to sounds. Those sounds are the words of your conversations. These devices can detect and distinguish the vibrations from separate voices even when people are talking at the same time."

"How long have they been here?" asked Callahan.

"It's hard to say. This technology has been around for a while, but these are the latest versions. And they are very, very expensive. They've not been on the market long. Less than a year," said Nick.

"Did you—"

Nick interrupted Callahan again. "Yes, I did. I checked all the windows in your house, and they're clean of listening devices. I thought you might want me to do that. I hope you don't mind," said Nick.

Callahan wondered, not for the first time, how Nick could anticipate what someone was going to say and either answer their unspoken question or complete their thought for them. He found it an annoying idiosyncrasy but fascinating. Nick was rarely wrong.

Callahan gestured toward the chair in front of his desk, and Nick sat down.

"What about the two women?" he asked.

Nick cleared his throat and then said, "They served time together at the Logan Correctional Center in Illinois, a prison for female offenders. They both received a college associate degree in computer science there." Nick reached into his back pocket and took out a folded wad of paper. He fumbled with it until he'd separated three sheets of paper. "My notes," he said.

"No offense, Nick, but for a techie isn't paper and pen a bit prehistoric? I was expecting to be dazzled with the latest in electronic presentation," said Callahan.

Nick glanced up from his notes with a worried look. "You're kidding. Right?" he said.

Callahan smiled.

Nick chuckled uneasily. "Oh, yes, of course," he said. "Moving on, things get interesting. Upon their release, they hooked up in Illinois for a time where they worked concessions at demolition derbies. After a while, they worked their way up and into the cars and begin participating in demolition, drag, and entry level circuit racing. Then they moved to LA. There, they become stunt drivers for TV. Their careers in high crime begin after that. There's apparently a vigorous market for getaway drivers, especially female."

"Who hired them?" asked Callahan.

Nicked squirmed in the chair and then sat up straight. "Here's how that worked," he began. "Criminals who specialize in high-skilled and high-paying crimes advertise their services on the dark web. So, I began my search there. Normally they don't do the advertising themselves. It's done through surrogates.

"These intermediaries find clients for those they represent, those who want violent, dangerous, or high-risk crimes committed. Payments for services rendered are made through these surrogates. The surrogates conceal their identities behind firewalls and by other protective measures. The criminals also mask their identities. Further, those who hire on the dark web disguise the source of their payments. Jobs get done and paid for, but no one knows who anyone is. Also, all communications are conducted through encrypted sites that eradicate communications within a set time. In other words, everything disappears and is virtually untraceable."

"So, we're at another damn dead end," said Callahan.

"Not necessarily. I discovered something. It's not what you were after, but it's critical and may involve Susan Gibbons' case." Nick paused.

"What did you find out?" asked Callahan.

"You need special software to gain entry to the dark web. I hacked the software, and then posed on the web as someone who needed a job done quickly that involved females with the skill set of our two women. Several surrogates with cloaked identities contacted me. They directed me to different encrypted sites and then asked for specifics. I described a job that required our women's exact skills and experience. One surrogate said that the pair I sought wasn't available. I suspected then that I'd flushed out their intermediary. From there, I tracked his or her presence on the web. It wasn't difficult. He or she surfed every site I'd been directed to.

"On one of those sites I came across an ad for a job that also had to be accomplished quickly." Nick folded his notes and stuck them back in his pocket without taking his eyes off Callahan. "The ad was incomprehensible to anyone outside of a select group that knows how to interpret it. I had to penetrate similar ads when I worked for the NSA and recognized it for what it was. You must submerge to the deepest levels of the dark web to gain entry. You undergo a vetting process before you're let in. I created a digital shadow that eventually passed muster. It took time, but, after several tries, I was successful."

"And what's the job?" asked Callahan.

"A contract has been placed on Bland's life. There's a bounty on his head. Someone is offering two million dollars to have him killed."

Chapter 85

W HEN ELIZABETH CHAMBERS ENTERED Callahan's office with
Bland, she instantly shoved the room's atmosphere into its
four corners and replaced it with her presence. With no preliminaries, she began beating a drumroll of conditions for the interview
and rearranging the seating in the office. She pulled the two chairs
facing Callahan's desk farther back into the room and positioned
them so one was to the side but in front of the other. She angled the
chairs toward the door, forcing Callahan and Amanda to move their
chairs around from behind the desk. She ordered Bland to sit in the
rear chair. She then assumed a commanding stance beside her client
and laid a protective hand on his shoulder. Amanda struggled to
stifle a laugh.

Chambers and her client were a study in contrasts. She posed, stat-
uesque, in a bone-white designer pantsuit. The partially unbuttoned
silk blouse under her slim-collared jacket revealed the glitter of a gold
necklace. A large diamond blinked on her left hand. The lattice of her

black sandals dressed two ranks of perfectly pedicured ruby-red nails. And what did her billion-dollar client wear? Cargo shorts, a faded red t-shirt (torn at the neck), flipflops, and a three-day beard. They looked like the setup for a skit on *Saturday Night Live.*

"If we're all agreed to my stated conditions we can start; if not, this interview is over before it begins. My client is here voluntarily, so it's up to you." Chambers swiveled her head, looking first toward Callahan and then Amanda.

Amanda glanced over at Callahan with a look that said *What the hell?* and waited for him to react.

"Good morning, Miss Chambers. I hope you had a pleasant trip to the island. If you'll sit down, we can begin," said Callahan.

Chambers sat. "That's *Ms.*," she said, dragging the *s* out as a series of *z*'s.

"Certainly," said Callahan, opening the computer on his desk and turning it to face Chambers and Bland. "We're investigating the death of a Susan Gibbons, an island resident. We're going to show you a video that was taken by a deckhand on a tug in lake Michigan. Then I want to ask you some—"

"Hold on a minute, is my client implicated in her death?" interrupted Chambers.

"We believe he may be able to help us in our investigation. He is not a suspect at this time," said Callahan.

"You've already questioned him about her death. Why more questions now?" she persisted.

"We've recently discovered what may be evidence involving her death. We want to ask him what he knows about it, if anything," said Callahan.

When Chambers didn't respond, he said to Bland, "Please note the date and time imprinted on the video."

Bland nodded, and Callahan wormed the cursor to the play icon and clicked.

As the video began to play, both Bland and Chambers scooted their chairs closer to Callahan's desk. Neither said a word as the video continued.

When it ended, Callahan said to Bland, "You recognize the ship in this video, don't you?"

"Yes," said Bland. "It's the *Odyssey*."

"Do you recognize either of the two people captured in this video?' he asked.

"No. How could I? They're little more than shadows," answered Bland.

"Were you on the *Odyssey* at the time shown in this video?"

Chambers reached over and put her hand on Bland's arm to silence him.

"It's okay," he said to her; then to Callahan, "No. I wasn't."

"Where were you?" continued Callahan.

"As a matter of fact, I remember the date well. I was on Mackinac Island. I was a guest of the governor, one of several. I stayed in his summer residence there. I'm sure you can check with him or anyone on the guest list to verify it."

"Do you know who was on the *Odyssey* at the time shown in the video?"

"I have no idea. As far as I know, it was supposed to be at anchor in your harbor. Only crew members should have been on board. You're free to check the manifest, however."

"We have," said Callahan without elaborating. "The company that provides the ship's officers and crew is cooperating with our investigation," he added.

Amanda leaned over and whispered into Callahan's ear. When

she sat back up, he said, "Were you subsequently told, or did you hear or otherwise learn about anything that happened on the yacht that night?"

"No, as I've said, I thought it was in the harbor," answered Bland.

"He's told you he doesn't know anything about the yacht's passengers, whereabouts, or what may have happened on it that night. He wasn't on the ship or even the island. So, is there anything else, or are we done here?" said Chambers.

"There's one more thing," said Callahan.

Chambers slumped in her chair and sighed with exasperation. "What is it?" she said.

Callahan turned to her client. "Mr. Bland, there's a contract out on your life. Someone is willing to pay two million dollars to have you killed."

There were several moments of shocked silence. Bland's jaw literally dropped.

Then Chambers said, "Who? Who has put a contract out on him?"

"We don't know that," answered Callahan.

Chambers leaped from her chair and rushed at Callahan. She stopped a foot from his chair and bent over him, her arms at her side with fists clenched.

"Is this some goddamn ploy? Are you trying to scare my client into revealing incriminating information? Is that it?" she snarled.

"It's no ploy Ms. Chambers," said Callahan, looking up at her. "We have creditable information that your client's life is in imminent danger."

Bland mumbled something, stood up, and started walking out of the office. "I knew it," he said louder. "The son of a bitch wants me dead."

"Who wants you dead?" said Amanda, stepping in front of Bland to block his exit.

"Get out of my way," he said and pushed her aside.

Amanda started to follow him, but Callahan grabbed her arm. "Let him go," he said.

"If this is a stunt, Callahan, I'll have your badge," Chambers shouted over her shoulder as she trailed her client out of the station.

Chapter 86

THE WAR OF WORDS between Mrs. Hannity and the revelers at the Back Door had escalated. The two parties now employed missiles and explosives. Mrs. Hannity had taken to lobbing raw eggs at the cars parked on the road in front of her house. The revelers retaliated with fire crackers thrown in her front yard and on her porch in the dead of night. Heaven only knew when the guerrilla tactics would spiral into open warfare, thought Callahan. He wanted to put an end to the conflict before that happened, and he hoped he had the solution. It sat right next to him in the cruiser as he drove to Mrs. Hannity's property.

'You sure she's okay with this?" Seamus Kennedy leaned closer to the open window and let the stream of air blast his face for a few seconds. "And the county is on board?" he added.

"Absolutely, with respect to Mrs. Hannity," said Callahan. "She's anxious to talk to you. As far as the county's concerned, parking is legal day or night on the road in front of her house. So, it won't allow property owners to obstruct parking. However, a *No Parking* warning that qualifies as art . . . Callahan let Seamus come to his own conclusion on that one.

Seamus scratched the whiskers on his chin. "And I'm getting paid?" he asked just for reassurance.

"You are," answered Callahan.

"This is a sweet deal," said Seamus.

"It is, and it will promote your art," said Callahan.

"I was thinking of putting Elvis Presley and Michael Jackson on two benches on Mrs. Hannity's front lawn abutting the road. Beside them will be a working lamp post with a hanging sign that reads, *Photo Op, Do Not Block*," said Seamus, musing on the composition of his future work of art. "Only a clueless fool would block a view of Michael and Elvis. Anyway, no one's likely to park in front of the benches day or night because they'll want to look at or sit and have their pictures taken with sculptures of famous people and won't want the opportunity prevented by parked cars," added Seamus.

"That's the plan," said Callahan, having banked on Seamus's artistic talents being both brilliant and crafty.

*   *   *

Callahan parked the cruiser on the street by the gate that separated the public walkway from the ferry dock. The ferry had just rounded the southern tip of the bay and people were exiting their cars and entering the gate to greet arriving visitors. Passengers to the mainland began to mill about the boarding area. Julie, Max, and the dog were on the ferry; and he was excited to see them. Julie had not wanted to leave the island, but he had insisted, worried beyond reason about her and Max's safety after the kidnapping. Julie had put her foot down. Being shoved out of harm's way was no longer in the playbook. She was coming home, and there wasn't a damn thing he could do about it. Her job was on the island; he was on the island. It was where she belonged no matter what. But he still worried.

Whether the FBI's investigation could now garner enough evidence to indict Abdullah and Bland for financial crimes remained unclear. Even if it could, the legal maneuverings of the high-priced teams of lawyers that Abdullah and Bland could afford might stretch the proceedings into years. And, as far as Callahan knew, no extradition treaty existed between the UAE and the US, so Abdullah could hide out in perfect safety in Dubai.

Despite the kudos from Dempsey, the way he saw it, he had accomplished nothing. Two likely murderers and kidnappers were still free, and he believed one of them was in his county. He now felt convinced that Bland had Susan Gibbons and Jackson murdered or was covering up for whoever had. Susan Gibbons had died clutching a computer that appeared to contain encrypted data about the flow of money from Dubai through off-shore accounts to companies owned by Bland and into the coffers of politicians in the Michigan legislature, politicians whose votes could pass into law the pending bill allowing drilling for oil and natural gas in Lake Michigan.

Bland also owned stock in companies connected to secret drilling rigs along the Michigan shoreline. He and Abdullah stood to gain billions in the production of oil and natural gas from the lake if the bill succeeded, but not if their crimes were discovered. They thus had a motive for murder. They also had the opportunity: Susan Gibbons worked on the *Odyssey*, Bland's yacht, at the time of her death. The evidence inexorably pointed to Bland and Abdullah but inconclusively. The FBI had to connect solidly the source of the money to Abdullah and prove Bland's complicity in its illegal flow to members of the Michigan legislature.

And the video, although showing a murder, neither identified the victim nor the perpetrator. Callahan knew in his gut that Bland had lied about what he had seen in the video. Someone was in the act of murdering Susan Gibbons, and Bland knew who. His gut also told him that Bland would do whatever it took to protect the identity of that person, especially if he was that person.

As the ship approached the dock, Callahan saw Max standing on a bench in the bow holding the dog and waving to him. Julie held on to him with one hand and waved excitedly with the other, smiling. Callahan raised his hand to wave back, and, at that moment, all worry vanished.

Chapter 87

CALLAHAN LEANED ON THE cruiser's open door and watched the small airplane tow the banner over the beach. Swimmers, sunbathers, and picnickers all looked up as *PREVENT DRILLING IN THE LAKE. ACT NOW* sliced across the sky above them. Beneath the aerial entreaty glowed a website address. Someone had hired a fleet from Sky Media to fly up and down the eastern shore of Lake Michigan, and now it was the island's turn. The plane had been circling the island all afternoon buzzing the popular beaches.

Fred's Boat Rental on Rainbow Bay had submitted its annual application for a boat livery permit to the station. On his way to inspect Fred's motorized rental boats to ensure they met Michigan's safety standards, Callahan had stopped to view the plane.

The plane banked and was heading back over the beach when the cruiser's radio blared.

"Matt, you're wanted out at Bland's bunker immediately. Amanda's waiting for you there." Julie's voice crackled over the cruiser's transceiver and then went silent.

Callahan reached into the cruiser and grabbed the radio's mic. He keyed it. "What's going on?" he asked.

"Not sure. Bland called the station asking for you. Amanda was here so I gave her the call. She's out at the bunker and says Bland is inside and won't open the door until you're there. But he insisted that she stay until you arrived. He's very agitated, she said. Also, his security personnel are nowhere to be found. That's all I know," said Julie.

*   *   *

The door to the bunker opened before Callahan reached the end of the walkway to the entrance.

"Come in, please," said Bland, standing inside, out of sight behind the heavy door.

Callahan and Amanda entered, and Bland quickly pushed the door shut.

The immaculate and harmonized sunken living room that Amanda remembered now appeared disheveled. Dead flowers drooped in vases; food encrusted plates littered most of the flat surfaces of the room, including the seats of chairs; and an automatic rifle and ammunition lay across the cut-glass and marble table opposite the sprawling white leather couch. Bland looked haggard as he shambled to the couch and collapsed onto it. He slowly lowered his hand toward the floor for Callahan and Amanda to sit.

Amanda removed two plates from a chair and placed them on the floor. Then she sat down but not before she brushed off the cushion.

Callahan picked up the automatic rifle. "What's this about? And where is everyone?" he asked.

"I sent them away. I fired them. I don't trust them. I don't trust anybody," said Bland.

"So you've armed yourself?" said Callahan.

Bland nodded.

"Against what?" asked Callahan.

"I know who wants me dead. And he will succeed in killing me. He can get to anybody through anybody. I've seen him do it," said Bland.

"Who do you think is going to kill you?" asked Amanda leaning forward in her chair.

"I don't think. I know. It's Abdullah," answered Bland. He bent over, almost double, and covered his face with his hands. "I'm exhausted, I'm afraid, and I need help," he added.

"You want us to protect you?" Amanda sounded incredulous even to herself. "With all your money, you could hire an army to guard this place," she blurted out without thinking.

Bland dropped his hands and raised his head. He glared at Amanda. "Abdullah could buy me a hundred times over. One day soon I will simply be found dead from a drug overdose or drunk and drowned in my pool, or. . . At least those will appear to be the causes."

Callahan set the rifle back down on the table. "Then what do you want?" he asked.

Bland looked up a Callahan. "My money won't protect me, but I have something that will." Bland paused and then said, "Information. I have information. I know how Abdullah is growing his wealth. I know what he is doing with it and how. It's information the government wants and needs. I know that now. It's what Susan Gibbons was after. I know who killed her and who had that federal marshal killed. I know everything."

Amanda stood up. "Are you seeking protection from the government? Are you trying to enter the Witness Security Program?" Bland turned to her and sat upright, supporting himself with both hands on the cushions. "Abdullah wants me dead because he thinks I'm losing my nerve. I told him you were getting too close to us, finding out too much, that we should cut our losses, wash everything clean, and back out before you uncovered it all." Bland shook his head. "The collateral damage was getting too high."

Callahan lunged at Bland, grabbed him by his shirt, and yanked him to his feet. "You son of a bitch. You call multiple deaths and kidnapping collateral damage? You made your last mistake when you broke into my circle and messed with those inside it. The only help you'll get from us is escorting your body to the morgue." Callahan shoved Bland away. Bland fell back against the couch, lost his balance, and tumbled to the floor; landing on his side.

Callahan took the rifle from the table and signaled for Amanda to follow him as he headed for the door. "I hope we get that pleasure very soon," he said, reaching for the handle.

"This bunker has become my prison." Bland whined. "I need to disappear. You have to—" His last words were cut off as the steel door shut.

*　*　*

"Why did you take his rifle?" Amanda took the keys to the cruiser out of her pocket as she and Callahan walked from Bland's bunker.

"I want Bland to feel even more vulnerable than he does now. Plus, I don't want the asshole to shoot himself or anybody else before I can get Dempsey here to interrogate him," said Callahan.

"Then we're going to watch over him until that happens?" asked Amanda.

"Yep. You call Sheriff Markos and have him fly a couple of deputies out here to help us guard this place. I'll call Dempsey and tell him Bland wants to spill his guts for a price," said Callahan.

"The price being buried out of sight in the Witness Security Program?" Amanda tossed the keys in the air and then caught them.

"Sure looks that way," said Callahan.

Amanda reached for the door of the cruiser but stopped before she opened it. "You okay with that?" she asked.

"Maybe," answered Callahan. "We'll see."

Chapter 88

✪✪

THE HELICOPTER TOUCHED DOWN on the front lawn of the bunker and four armed FBI agents raced to the entrance and escorted Bland from the door to the chopper at a run. As the helicopter lifted off the ground, Dempsey gave Callahan a quick salute from its window.

Chapter 89

CALLAHAN GATHERED AMANDA, NICK, and Julie in his office. Dempsey had called him earlier with the status on Bland. He had important news to tell them.

"Congratulations are definitely in order," he began. "Bland turned out to be a treasure trove. Turning him will help bring down one of the largest human trafficking syndicates in the world and impound its fortune. Through Bland, the Justice Department now has solid evidence to prosecute and convict those running the syndicate. Bland is now under deep cover in the Witness Security Program.

"According to Bland's testimony, Abdullah served as the syndicate's money man and routed billions from its operations in Thailand to Dubai. As we thought, from there, he laundered huge chunks of the money through Bland's companies where it found its way into the pockets of members of the Michigan legislature. Bland and Abdullah wanted to influence the vote on the bill allowing drilling for oil and gas in Lake Michigan. They had already bought up land in key areas of the lakeshore for that purpose. As fallout from this, seven Michigan congresspersons are going to prison along with the governor. They did not report the money they pocketed to the IRS."

"What about Abdullah?" interrupted Amanda. "Can't he escape prosecution here by staying in Dubai?"

"Yes and no," said Callahan. "There is no extradition treaty between the United Arab Emirates and the United States, but it appears that Abdullah is not one of the most popular princes. He and his family have alienated those who hold real power in the Emirates. They want to get rid of him to stay on good terms with our government, so he's being sent here. He'll be arrested when he arrives."

"And what about— " Nick began to speak.

"Susan Gibbons?" Callahan turned the tables for once on Nick and completed his question. "I was saving her for last. Abdullah murdered her. According to Bland, Abdullah was only in Thailand once with high level members of the syndicate, but Susan must have recognized him on the yacht. He found her searching his computer and murdered her. When Abdullah found out about Jackson's affair with her, apparently by bugging our office, he had him killed." Before anyone could ask another question, Callahan slapped his hands on his desk. "That's it then," he said. Let's get back to work."

As everyone was leaving, he touched Julie's arm and motioned for her to stay. When they were alone, he said, "It's over now. We've nothing to fear anymore."

*   *   *

Julie received a call about a stray dog on the bay's public beach. Callahan was on his way to the cruiser to answer the call when a young man on a bicycle rode onto the station's gravel driveway and stopped in front of Callahan. He swung off the bike and extended his hand across the handlebars in greeting to Callahan.

"Good morning, Sheriff. I'm Edward Chen, the new editor of the *Ledger* now that Mr. Gallagher's retired. I was hoping you'd be at the station."

Callahan shook his hand. "Good to meet you," he said. "What can I do for you?"

"Well, I'm researching a story and am looking for Anthony Bland. I've been out to his place here on the island several times but he's not there, and no one seems to know where he is. I thought you might know where I can find him."

Callahan's thin smile widened until it grew into a full-blown grin. "I have absolutely no earthly idea," he said. "And you can quote me on that."

THE END

AUTHOR'S NOTE

Michigan's Natural Resources and Environmental Protection Act provides in part as follows:

The supervisor of mineral wells, acting directly or through his or her deputy or authorized representative, may do any of the following:

(d) Require on all wells the keeping and filing of logs containing data that are appropriate to the purposes of this part. Logs on brine and test wells shall be held confidential for 10 years after completion and shall not be open to public inspection during that time except by written consent of the owner or operator. Logs for test wells drilled for exploratory purposes shall be held confidential until released by the owner or operator. The logs on all brine and test wells for exploratory purposes shall be opened to public inspection when the owner is no longer an active mineral producer, mineral lease holder, or owner of mineral lands in this state.

*

In 1953, the state of Michigan granted an underwater easement through the Straits of Mackinac for an oil pipeline running from shale oil wells in Canada to oil refineries in Detroit. That pipe line, known as line 5, is still active. As of the printing of this book, it has never leaked.

Acknowledgments

I want to express a special thanks to Dr. Michael Kaufman for his medical knowledge, keen editing, enthusiasm, and friendship, all of which I gratefully relied on in completing this novel.

As always, my thanks to Don Debruin, John Morris, Robert Karrow, Kriste Masek, Colleen Seal, Carrie Munno, Patti Cone, Gary Strokosch, and Jonathan Alpert for once again diving in and reading the manuscripts of this work and for the invaluable feedback they gave.

And to Joan—editor and helpmate supreme.

About the Author

Russell Fee grew up in Washington, D.C. and London. After graduating from the College of William and Mary, he served in the army as a military intelligence officer and then became a trial lawyer, litigating civil rights and civil liberties cases, before becoming a teacher. In their inimitable ways, these careers inspired his novels and book of poetry. He and his wife have traveled the world and are dual citizens of the United States and Ireland. They now live in the Midwest, which they both love.